The Ellie's War series:

ELLIE'S WAR
The Final Ashes

EMILY SHARRATT

SCHOLASTIC

Scholastic Children's Books
An imprint of Scholastic Ltd
Euston House, 24 Eversholt Street, London, NW1 1DB, UK
Registered office: Westfield Road, Southam, Warwickshire, CV47 0RA
SCHOLASTIC and associated logos are trademarks and/or
registered trademarks of Scholastic Inc.

First published in the UK by Scholastic Ltd, 2016

Text copyright © Scholastic Ltd, 2016

The right of Emily Sharratt to be identified as the
author of this work has been asserted by her.

ISBN 978 1407 14499 3

A CIP catalogue record for this book
is available from the British Library.

Printed by CPI Group (UK) Ltd, Croydon, CR0 4YY
Papers used by Scholastic Children's Books are made
from wood grown in sustainable forests.

This is
and dialo   ed
fictitio

For my mum and dad,
who reared me on stories – E.S.

ONE

FEBRUARY, 1918

Ellie brushed her hands over the young soldier's eyes,
closing them for the final time. For a moment she
imagined she could feel his eyelashes tickling her palm
as they moved, but she knew that was impossible now.
She pulled the bedsheet up and smoothed it over his
skinny chest. Her own eyes were dry, but her hand
trembled ever so slightly as she gave his fingers one last
squeeze.

Finally she looked up and met the eyes of the white-
haired doctor whom she had been assisting. He smiled
kindly at her. "It doesn't get any easier, does it?"

She shook her head in reply.

"I don't think it would be right if it did. But you helped me make him comfortable at the end, my dear, and for that I am very grateful. I'm sure his family would be too. I believe you may return to your own ward now; things appear to be settling down here somewhat."

"Yes, Doctor."

As Ellie walked back through the main ward towards the stairs, she saw that he was right. A few hours previously, she and other nurses working in the less critical wards around the hospital had been called to help with the sudden influx of new and critically injured patients. As usual, the scenes on their arrival would have struck the untrained eye as nightmarish and chaotic, but after more than a year working there, Ellie knew better. The hospital was a complex structure of strictly maintained systems, with a large staff of experienced doctors and nurses, as well as volunteers such as Ellie. It was an efficient machine. Unfortunately, there seemed to be no end to the supply of injured and dying soldiers needing treatment; it had begun to appear as though the war truly would go on for ever.

Ellie knew she ought to hurry back to her own ward, where her usual patients and tasks would be waiting for her, but she couldn't bring herself to rush. Death, however often she faced it – and she saw it on a daily basis in the hospital – *didn't* get any easier to accept. Her mind kept drifting back to the young soldier; unlike her own patients, she didn't know anything about him. But he would have a family and friends somewhere who would miss him maybe a sweetheart or even a fiancée. Surely England would soon run out of young men to be sent away to die?

"Ellie!"

She looked up with a start; her friend and colleague Grace Fletcher was hurrying down the stairs towards her. As always, Grace's uniform seemed to fit her so much more elegantly than anybody else's: even the flat blue colour served to highlight the vibrant shade of her eyes. It was impossible to resent her, though; almost impossible to keep from smiling when Grace was around.

"There you are! Come on, you're needed."

Ellie stopped dead in the middle of the stairs. "Why, what's wrong?"

Grace laughed as she drew level with Ellie, and then pressed her hand to her mouth. "I'm sorry, I shouldn't make fun, but you look so stricken! Nothing's wrong; we just need you for a job back upstairs." She narrowed her eyes as though trying to detect something hidden beneath the surface of Ellie's skin. "Are you all right? Have you just had a grim time of things downstairs?" She threaded her arm through Ellie's and began to escort her up the stairs.

"I'm fine, really. Nothing compared to what the girls down there have to cope with. It was just a patient that we weren't able to save."

"Oh, I'm sorry, love." Grace stopped again, her eyes still roving over the younger girl's face. "Hmmm, maybe now isn't the time..."

"What is it? Something *has* happened, hasn't it? I knew it..."

"No, no," Grace shushed her, no trace of a smile now. "Look, it was supposed to be a surprise, but I think perhaps you've had enough of those for one day. We were just waiting for you to return so we could have a little tea to celebrate your birthday."

"Oh!" In all the busyness of the past couple of hours,

Ellie had completely forgotten about her birthday. Now she thought about it, Grace *had* been acting rather suspiciously earlier on in the day.

"We don't have to, if you don't feel up to it. I can go and tell the others..."

"No, I'd like to." Ellie chewed at her lip. "Does that seem awful?"

"Of course not! We all have to keep our spirits up somehow. And it's not every day you turn seventeen. Come on!"

As they walked into the ward, they were greeted by a cheer from the men, propped up in their beds around the room. Ellie instantly felt her eyes sting at the sight of the equipment trolley, relieved of its usual burden of bandages, bedpans and syringes, and instead standing resplendent with small bunches of snowdrops in jam jars, a pot of tea, a milk jug and dainty china cups that someone must have brought from home, and one sticky bun in pride of place. Waiting by the trolley was Ellie's Aunt Frances, in an apron so clean she must have only just changed it, and – Ellie's eyes widened – the ferocious matron of the hospital.

Matron herself began to lead the others in a rousing

rendition of "For She's a Jolly Good Fellow", and Grace joined in in ringing tones while never loosening her grip on Ellie's arm. Ellie felt herself flush with pleasure.

Afterwards the nurses perched on the ends of the beds while Grace poured and distributed the tea. Ellie wanted to share her bun with everyone – with rationing, such a treat was rare for all of them – but eventually had to concede that it would be reduced to crumbs if she tried to split it sixteen ways. Instead, she contented herself with slipping morsels of it to Aunt Frances, whom she was sure had been having an unpleasant time of it downstairs. Her attention kept being drawn back to the implications of that fresh apron.

"Are you really only seventeen, Nurse Phillips?" Private Bryson was asking her now. "You seem such a professional I thought you must have been working here for years."

Ellie smiled, at the same time casting a nervous glance at Matron, who did not like excessive praise to be offered too freely to any of her nurses. "Thank you, that's kind of you to say so. But, yes, I'm seventeen today."

"So young," murmured Private Lessing. He himself

was no more than nineteen and had lost a foot following an infected wound. He said it quietly, but clearly Ellie wasn't the only one who had heard him.

"Yes, Private, Nurse Phillips is young, but I knew she was up to the job when I took her on. I trust I am allowed to make the decisions on the hiring of staff for my hospital."

Ellie and Grace exchanged a glance and then hurriedly looked away before they burst out laughing. Poor Private Lessing flushed a deep shade of red. Not even the most formidable doctors in the hospital dared to challenge Matron.

"Shall we have a bit of a singalong?" Grace ventured.

Matron looked thoughtfully at Private Lessing. In the month that he had been in the hospital it had come to the attention of his fellow patients and some of the staff that, despite his shyness, he had a beautiful singing voice: sweet but powerful. Since then, few could miss an opportunity to hear him sing.

"Well, we all ought to be getting back to work, but I dare say one song won't hurt, to send us on our way in good spirits. Private Lessing, you are our choirmaster. What will it be?"

Private Lessing ducked his head and wrung his bedsheets nervously between his hands. "Nurse Phillips ought to choose, as it is her birthday."

Ellie nodded at him encouragingly. "What about 'You're in Style When You're Wearing a Smile'?" she suggested, naming her current favourite from the wireless.

Everyone agreed and Private Lessing led them in, his rich, clear voice helping to smooth the many discordant ones in the gathering – including Matron's.

As was often the case, Aunt Frances had to work later than her niece, so Ellie walked home from the hospital by herself that afternoon. There was a biting February wind and the sun was low in the sky, ringing the clouds with lines of fire as it descended. Ellie pulled her coat closely about her and tucked her gloved hands under her arms. She could barely take her eyes from the sky; the colours were mesmerizing.

Reaching the door to the digs in which she and Aunt Frances lived, Ellie puffed out one last steamy breath, and then closed it firmly behind her. She peeled off her gloves, pulling repeatedly on each finger to loosen them first. As she did so, so she noticed an envelope propped against the carriage clock on the hallway table, her friend Jack's familiar, careful handwriting creeping across it, and smiled.

As she was fumbling impatiently with the buttons of her coat, her landlady, Mrs Joyce, walked out to greet her. "Happy birthday, my dear. There's a fish chowder on the stove for you as a special treat."

"Oh, thank you, Mrs Joyce. That's so kind of you." Mrs Joyce's fish chowder was one of Ellie's favourite meals.

"Not at all, my dear, not at all. You enjoy that. I just have to run down the road to check in on old Mrs Parkin, but I'll be back to have a cup of tea with you later on."

Ellie smiled. She was very fond of Mrs Joyce, who in many ways was more maternal than her own mother had ever been, but still she was glad to be able to read Jack's letter on her own over dinner.

She changed hurriedly out of her uniform, washed her hands, and was soon seated at the kitchen table, a steaming bowl of Mrs Joyce's fine chowder before her. This recipe, like so many others the landlady followed, Ellie knew, came from *The Win-the-War Cookery Book*, and was designed to make their rations go as far as possible.

Unable to wait any longer, Ellie tore at the envelope. At first her eyes roved over the page, unable read it through properly, instead picking up disjointed phrases here and there:

Happy birthday, Ellie!

... wish I could see you on your seventeenth birthday. I still remember your seventh!

... will take Charlie down to our tree in the woods after work to have a pretend birthday tea party and play some songs on my fiddle...

We left some fresh snowdrops the other day in the place where you and I buried your dad's things...

Charlie is missing you a lot ... think your mam must be too, though of course she doesn't say. I know I am!

... can't wait to see you next month...

Ellie took a spoonful of chowder – still hot enough to scald her tongue – then smoothed the paper down and began to read carefully from start to finish.

It was strange; her life here in Brighton was so engrossing and, for the most part, she was very content. When she didn't think about home, about the people she missed so much, she could almost imagine that she wasn't homesick – that she was an entirely different Ellie, one with no attachments to the small village of Endstone in Kent.

Jack's letters destroyed that illusion. But, still, she was always happy to receive them. It made him feel not quite so far away.

She would be going home to Endstone next month. She hadn't been back since Christmas, and these days every visit seemed to bring a fresh shock. There were no able-bodied men over the age of eighteen left in the village at all now. The central square bore the ugly scars of the bombing the previous summer, and the people were still recovering from such devastation in their midst, as well as from the loss of Sarah Pritchard, who had been killed.

Charlie is missing you a lot ... think your mam must be too, though of course she doesn't say.

It was Ellie's instinct to snort as she reread the line

about her mother, but she fought it. Jack was right; in recent years her mother's behaviour towards her had softened. It seemed she had even come to think that she might need her daughter.

Ellie tore a strip from the single slice of bread the rationing allowed her and popped it into her mouth as she imagined Jack and Charlie under her favourite oak tree in the woods – the one with so many happy memories of both her father and of childhood games with Jack.

She smiled. She and Jack had been friends through most of the birthdays they had ever had. Jack would be eighteen at his next...

The piece of bread felt as though it had turned to paper in her mouth. She took a messy slurp of water to force it down. Eighteen. The age he had once longed to be, back when he had wanted more than anything to be a soldier, to go away to war with her father and his older brother, and the other men of the village.

Of course, he knew better now. Even Ellie could not have anticipated how much his time on the front line – after he had run away and lied about his age – would change him.

But when Jack turned eighteen there would no longer be any choice in the matter. He was strong and healthy; even the leg that had been injured in the explosion at the munitions factory now gave him no more than a twinge in the cold weather.

No, there was no question but that he would be called up. Just four months to go. After all these years, could there be any hope that the war would end in time to prevent it?

TWO

MARCH

As Ellie neared the top of the hill that led up to her home, she began to run. Her legs strained against the increased incline and the cold air tore the breath from her lungs, but still she was smiling. She raced up to the door – pausing to note that the front garden was looking very overgrown – and pushed it open.

"Eleanor!" Her mother was already standing in the hallway as though waiting for her.

Oh! Ellie thought. *Maybe she was waiting for me.* "Mother," she replied, dropping her bag and stepping forward to give her a kiss on the cheek.

She felt Mother's hand grasp her shoulder, the grip

tremulous. As ever, her mother's pallor and frailness were a shock to Ellie. But her smile seemed heartfelt, and made her appear younger.

"How are you, Mo—"

"Ellie!"

Ellie broke off and grinned up the stairs at her brother's form, which looked so much longer and less rounded since she had last seen him. "Come down here, Charlie boy, and give your big sister a hug."

Charlie pulled a face but trotted obediently down the stairs and into Ellie's arms. She wrapped them tightly around him, squeezing her eyes closed and breathing in his smell. It was to her – simply – *home*.

Charlie suffered this embrace for a long moment before patting her gently but firmly on the back in a way that clearly signified that he had had enough.

Ellie stood up laughing, though she had to rub her coat sleeve against her eyes, and noticed that Mother's eyelids were rather pink too.

"Shall we have a cup of tea?" she asked brightly, tousling Charlie's curls with her hand.

"Yes, let's," agreed Mother. "I've made some broth too, if you're hungry."

They wandered into the kitchen and Ellie busied herself about the stove while Mother and Charlie sat down at the table. There had been a time when such domestic tasks had been stiflingly boring to Ellie. Now they felt like a rare dose of home life.

"Are you well, Mother?" Ellie asked hopefully as she ladled the broth into three bowls.

"No worse than usual," Mother replied. "I continue to be very tired all the time, and my headaches are as bad as ever. Of course, with poor Sarah Pritchard gone, I get little help with Charlie these days, so I cannot afford to indulge my tiredness."

Ellie glanced guiltily at her as she stirred the tea leaves in the pot. Sarah Pritchard had been her mother's main support since Ellie's move to Brighton. She suspected that, in addition to the loss on a practical level, her mother was missing the young Belgian woman's companionship and cheerful disposition.

"Are you still attending the WI meetings?" she went on, bringing the bowls to the table. It had been such a pleasant surprise to her when Mother had started to involve herself in the village knitting group – which had then evolved into a Women's Institute branch – at the start of the war, making friends with some of the women of the village for the first time.

"Well, no," said Mother, with a touch of her old impatience. "It is difficult to bring Charlie now that he is bigger, and always running everywhere and climbing everything. And with no one else to take care of him. . ."

Ellie winced. "Do you still see any of the other women?"

Mother paused. "I see them at church, when I'm well enough to go. Sometimes Mrs Anderson will bring groceries up to me, when she is not too busy with little Arthur or with her vegetable-growing for the WI."

Ellie sat motionless, her spoon hovering above her bowl. It was just too hard. She knew how important her work in the hospital was, but how could she justify leaving her family when they were unable to cope without her? A dull ache began in the back her head.

Mother seemed to collect herself, and with visible effort, asked, "How is your work? Have you been given any new tasks on the ward?"

Ellie felt her face soften in response to this small kindness. There had been a time when Mother had seemed to think that Ellie's only role in life was to help her in the house and prepare herself for a good marriage. It was a mark of how Mother had changed that she was now showing interest in Ellie's work.

"It is good, thank you. Tiring but so rewarding." She handed Charlie a napkin to catch the broth that had escaped his spoon and trickled down his face, while rummaging through her mind for the best stories to tell her mother. She had to be quite selective; Mother would not like to hear anything she might think of as vulgar or mischievous; nothing too sad either. Ellie longed to speak of how she thought Private Lessing was in love with Grace – he blushed to the roots of his red hair whenever their eyes met and she thought the pretty nurse might be fond of him too, but sensed that Mother would not approve.

In the end, she settled for the story of a young private who had been discharged a week previously. Having suffered a serious injury to the head, he had lost the use of his right eye, and would not be returning to the front, but rather heading back home to his family in London. These days, it felt as though that was the best any soldier on the battlefields in Europe could hope for.

*

After lunch, Ellie persuaded Mother to go for a lie-down while she cleared up the bowls from their meal. She ushered Charlie into the front garden to get some fresh air where she could keep an eye on him through the kitchen window. As she filled the washing basin with water, her mind continued to roll around the problem of how she could take care of Mother and Charlie, while not ending up stuck in Endstone for ever, and giving up on her own hopes and plans.

She rinsed the last bowl and then glanced out of the window in time to see Thomas Pritchard walking up the garden path. It made her heart contract painfully to see how his clothes hung off him, his eyes looking as though they had sunk deep into his head. Even his limp appeared more pronounced. It had been wonderful to watch how Thomas had been changed by his relationship with Sarah, seeming to grow stronger and brighter with his happiness. But the process in reverse was devastating to witness.

Ellie ran to the front door, trying to adopt a convincing smile, and pulled it open just as Thomas stopped to pass Charlie his ball.

"Ellie!" Thomas said in surprise.

"Thomas," she replied. As he walked up to greet her, she reached out and took hold of one of his hands between both of her own.

"I had forgotten your mother said you would be home. It's good to see you."

"And you," Ellie responded, flinching a little at the untruth: seeing him like this was so very distressing. "Please, come in."

Thomas followed her through the hallway and into the kitchen. "I've brought your mother the tablets for her headache."

"Thank you. You are good to bring them round when you're so busy," Ellie replied, setting the kettle on to the stove and reaching out to take the bottle of tablets so that she might read the label.

Thomas smiled. "Do you approve of my prescription, Nurse? I've moved her on to a higher dosage since I'm afraid the headaches appear to be getting worse."

Ellie felt her face burning. "Oh, I'm sorry – I wouldn't dream of questioning your judgement, Thomas. I suppose I'm just interested these days, now that I know a little more about it all myself."

"I'm pleased to see it," he replied with another

small smile, covering her hand with his own. "You're an intelligent young lady and I have no doubt you're turning into a very fine nurse indeed, Ellie."

She shifted uncomfortably then returned to the stove to pour water from the kettle into the teapot. "Thank you – you're kind to say so. But never mind me" – she turned back to face him – "how are you, Thomas?"

The young doctor's eyes dropped to the table. "Oh, I'm fine, really..."

"Thomas..." Putting the teapot onto the table and sitting down in front of him, it was Ellie's turn to take his hand. It was a long moment before he looked up to meet her eyes, and when he did, she saw his were bloodshot.

"I miss her, that's all," he said at last, his voice hoarse. "It's odd, really, when you think about it... Three years ago, I'd never even met her. If it hadn't been for the war, I never would have done. So ... so, you see, even though the war took her away from me, I can't—" He broke off and clamped his eyes tightly shut, his chin trembling slightly.

Ellie didn't trust herself to speak either. She sat

squeezing his hand, waiting as he sucked in deep, shaky breaths. Apart from Charlie's chatter floating in through the kitchen window, the house was silent.

Eventually Thomas opened his eyes again and gave her a half smile. "I'm sorry."

"Don't!" Ellie cried. "Don't be silly. You have nothing to apologize for. You know you're like family to me, Thomas. I just wish..." She trailed off and they stared levelly at each other. There was no need to say what they both wished. "How are the Mertens family?" she asked, pulling her hand back from his so that she could pour the tea into the cups.

"Oh." Thomas drew out his handkerchief and blew his nose. "Haven't you heard? They've gone to Whitstable to join Dr Mertens' sister and her family, who have been living there since fleeing Belgium. I think, after what happened, staying in Endstone was too hard. They just wanted to be around family, I suppose."

"That's perfectly understandable," Ellie said carefully. "But you must miss them, Thomas?"

"I do," he agreed, rubbing his eyes wearily with the heel of one hand and lifting his teacup with the other, "very much so. It makes me feel even more as though the whole thing were just something I dreamed. I will go and visit them there, though, when things settle down. If they ever do, that is..."

"Of course!" Ellie exclaimed, the thought only just occurring to her. "You must be struggling without Dr Mertens in the surgery!" *And without Sarah*, she added in her head, thinking of how much Thomas's wife had helped with the running of the practice, even before they had been married.

"I am. With more and more men returning injured from the front and requiring ongoing care, it's busier than ever. I'm getting very worried about these reports of influenza from Europe. And, if I'm honest, I'm just not on top of things in the way I need to be. I can't seem to get myself organized." Thomas stared into his teacup as though expecting to find the answers at the bottom of it

"No one could blame you for that, Thomas."

"In fact," he went on, almost as if he hadn't heard her, "I've been thinking about you, Ellie."

"*Me?*" she said, unable to keep the note of surprise out of her voice.

"Yes. Have you given any thought to how long you'll stay in Brighton?"

"Well, yes," she replied, her mind returning to the puzzle she had been pondering earlier. "I *have* thought about it. But I'm not sure what the answer is. I know Mother and Charlie need me here, but I feel I can really help at the hospital. . ."

"Of course. Your matron is very pleased with you."

"Is she?" Once again, Ellie was taken aback.

"Yes, she wrote to me." Thomas glanced at her face and gave a small laugh. "Ellie, you look stunned."

"I *am* stunned!"

"She wrote to me after Sarah died – you or Frances must have told her, I suppose?" Ellie nodded mutely. "Well, she sent me a very kind letter. And in it she mentioned how hard you were working, and that she felt you were becoming a very skilled nurse, with good instincts. She was very complimentary about my training – which I didn't feel I deserved at all!"

Again, Ellie couldn't speak.

"Anyway, I have no doubt that you are much valued there. But if you ever did wish to return to Endstone, there would be a job waiting for you if you wanted it – a real job as a nurse, I mean, not just helping out with odds and ends as you used to do." He peered at her face. "There is no pressure, you understand? I just wanted to make sure you realize that it's one option that exists for you."

"Thank you, Thomas," Ellie said quickly, conscious that, in her confusion, she probably appeared rude. "That is very good to know. And very kind of you. May I take some time to think about it?"

"Absolutely – you *must*, Ellie. You should take all the time you need. It was your father's surgery; it's not going anywhere and you will *always* be welcome."

"Thank you," Ellie said again. 'Thank you." She paused. "And, Thomas, would you mind not mentioning this conversation to Mother – just until I've thought about it some more?"

"Of course not; I understand," Thomas said sympathetically. He knew Ellie's mother well by now and could no doubt imagine her concerns. "Anyway," he said, rapping his knuckles on the table decisively, "I should be getting back to the surgery. Do call in to see me before you go back to Brighton, won't you?"

"I will. Thanks again, Thomas," Ellie said as they both stood. "Take care of yourself."

He smiled in reply before tugging his coat back on.

As she waved him off at the front door, Ellie saw Jack pulling up on his bicycle, hair springing out from under his cap, cheeks pink from the wind, and her stomach seemed to flip over.

Thomas and Jack spoke for a moment at the gate while Ellie jiggled impatiently on the doorstep, waiting until Thomas had turned away and walked out of view before racing to meet Jack halfway down the garden path and flinging her arms around him. She felt Jack's arm slide about her waist in response, his breath in her hair. Ellie tried for a moment to imagine how Thomas must feel, knowing that he would never be able to stand with his arms around Sarah, but her body seemed to rebel against the thought. She gave a violent shudder and squeezed Jack all the more tightly until he gave a gasping laugh.

"Steady on, El. I might need those ribs again!"

THREE

Since Ellie's mother was more accepting of his presence these days, Jack had stayed for dinner, enjoying the stew that Ellie had made, then doing the dishes while she settled Charlie down in bed. Now they were strolling hand in hand down the hill towards the village square. Jack had insisted he was going to buy her a belated birthday drink.

As they crossed the square, Ellie's eye was drawn to the cobbles in front of the village store, still scarred from the bomb that had landed there eight months previously. The damage to the store itself had been fixed, and the shop was up and running again under the expert management of Jack's mother and his sister, Anna, though of course at this time in the evening it was closed.

Ellie shyly withdrew her hand from Jack's as they walked into the smoky fug of the Dog and Duck pub. He grinned and winked. There was no question that the pub was quieter than it would have been in previous years; now the clientele mostly consisted of old men, injured veterans, factory workers too young to have been conscripted and the occasional woman – mostly land girls in from a hard day's farming in the countryside around Endstone. They called out greetings to Ellie as she and Jack made their way to the bar, as well as questions about Brighton and her work in the hospital, and how long she would be home this time.

At the bar, Vera Baker, the landlady, was pulling pints while shouting instructions to her young daughter, Maud, whom Ellie glimpsed peeking up from the cellar, her blue eyes glinting from deep in the gloom.

"Ah, Ellie Phillips, it's good to see you back, lass," Mrs Baker declared.

"Thank you, Mrs Baker, it's nice to be home."

"You haven't forgotten us all now you're living your exciting life in the big city?"

"Of course not!" Ellie said, feeling Jack's eyes on her.

"She'd better not," he put in, letting out his booming laugh.

"Ah well, I'm sure she won't be forgetting her handsome beau!" Mrs Baker laughed, giving a wink that instantly painted crimson splashes on Jack's cheeks. "What can I get you both?"

While she pulled their glasses of cider, the conversation turned to rationing, which had officially been introduced a few weeks previously, though shortages had existed for some time already.

Old Mr Thompson, the boys' teacher from the local school, was sitting up at the bar with a pint of stout and a newspaper. He greeted Ellie, and then asked, "I imagine you've received your ration cards in Brighton too, Eleanor?"

"Yes," Ellie replied, "though my landlady has mine since she does all the shopping for the house."

"Landlady!" cooed Mrs Baker. "You're a proper working girl now, aren't you? A real professional!"

Ellie smiled.

"Indeed she is," Mr Thompson proclaimed. "We

should probably be addressing you as Nurse Phillips these days, shouldn't we?"

"No, no," Ellie said. "'Ellie' will do just as well as it ever did! Besides, my matron wouldn't like to think I was giving myself airs and graces because I'm out from under her nose for a few days!"

The others chuckled.

"Well," Mrs Baker went on, "I know we must all do our bit, and heaven knows food supplies aren't what they were, but it's torture how little bread we're allowed now. This barley business is just not the same. And as for that so-called turnip bread..." She made a disgusted face that caused Ellie to pull her drink away from her mouth quickly before she spluttered into it. Jack sniggered and shook his head, passing her a handkerchief, which she used to dab at her mouth.

"Indeed," Mr Thompson said, "and it makes you think – if the government are having to introduce such measures, they can't be imagining that there is an end to the whole sorry affair in sight. Perhaps they're even anticipating tougher times ahead."

"Tougher?" Mrs Baker's jolly face fell, and Ellie

noticed for the first time how much thinner and more tired she was looking than the last time she had seen her. "Surely not?"

It was so strange to think that a couple of years ago it was Mrs Baker's husband working behind the bar, while she made sandwiches in the kitchen, changed the barrels, or was at home with their children; even stranger to think how they all just got on with their lives despite their terrible losses.

Mrs Baker was called away to serve another customer at the same time as Mr Thompson was drawn into conversation with the young veteran beside him. Jack took hold of Ellie's elbow and muttered into her ear, "Come on, El. Let's go and sit somewhere a bit quieter." She smiled back at him, only just restraining herself from reaching out to tuck one of his curls behind his ears.

Their glasses of cider in hand, they wound their way to a corner by the window – though not before Ellie had stopped to chat with several more villagers full of questions about her life in Brighton and stories of their own to tell.

It was always so comforting to be around people

that she had known for her whole life; to see the familiar faces and move around places that she would be confident navigating with her eyes closed. As she and Jack settled into their seats, Ellie allowed herself to think for a moment about what it would be like if she accepted Thomas's offer and moved back to Endstone permanently.

"Jack," she blurted, before she could decide whether it was a good idea, "Thomas said the most extraordinary thing to me today."

Jack was smiling as his eyes roamed fondly over her face. "Oh really? What *extraordinary thing* was that, then?"

She wrinkled her nose at his impersonation of her voice, then took a breath and chewed her lip before answering more slowly, "Well, he's obviously struggling on his own in the surgery. He ... he asked me if I'd like to work with him there."

"El!" Jack exclaimed, leaning forward and seizing her hand so suddenly that he almost tipped over his cider, rescuing it just in time. "Oops," he said with a grin, dabbing at the few spilled drops with his palm. "But, El, that's wonderful! You clever thing! I can't believe you waited so long to say anything – you must have been in agonies over dinner! This is just the chance we've been waiting for!"

Ellie felt her brow furrow slightly. "Well, yes, I mean ... I know it's a great offer."

Jack beamed at her. "Yes? You sound as though you're about to say 'but'."

"Yes, *but* I haven't given him an answer yet."

"What?" He looked utterly baffled now, one eyebrow raised questioningly, though still the smile was fixed in place. "Why ever not?"

"Well, because I haven't deci—"

"Hello, Jack!" came a voice from above them.

Ellie looked up, startled, and saw a pretty, dark-haired girl of around her own age standing over them. She'd been so engrossed in their conversation that she hadn't even seen her approach. The girl looked familiar, as most people from the village did, but Ellie couldn't place her.

"Maggie!" Jack said, smiling. "What are you doing here?"

"Same thing you are, I expect," Maggie responded, standing with her weight on her left leg so that her right hip jutted out. Her dimples were like pins in a pin cushion, Ellie thought.

"Maggie, this is my ... my very good friend, Ellie Phillips," Jack said, with an uncharacteristically shy smile. "El, this is Maggie Brown. We work together at the factory."

"Nice to meet you," Ellie said, still looking fixedly at the other girl.

"Likewise," Maggie said in a monotone, barely glancing in Ellie's direction. "Anyway, where did you dash off to after our shift, Jack? You were gone before I'd got out of my overalls!"

Ellie looked curiously at Jack, whose cheeks were glowing with their tell-tale red stripes again.

"Oh, sorry," he replied with a nervous chuckle. "I didn't mean to leave without saying goodbye, but I wanted to make sure I caught the earlier train. Ellie got back from Brighton today, you see. She's never home for long, so I have to make the most of it when she is – don't I, El?"

Maggie gave Ellie a longer look now. One eyebrow inched upwards, as though amused by what she saw, but all she said was, "I see."

Ellie felt her own eyes narrow. Who was this girl? And why was she now launching into a story – complete with raucous laughter – about the factory foreman, after Jack had just told her he wanted to make the most of their time together? Her timing couldn't have been worse; Ellie was wondering if she shouldn't have mentioned the job in the Endstone surgery to Jack yet. Clearly it hadn't occurred to him that she might not take it. She hadn't decided how she felt about it herself yet. Of course, in many ways it would solve all the problems she had been struggling with – and she was hugely flattered to be considered good enough for the job – but Brighton had been such an adventure. She'd experienced such freedom living and working away from home. She was learning so much every day at the hospital, as well as making a real difference to the lives of the soldiers. Matron and the other staff had gone out of their way to accommodate her when she was still young – she thought again with a flush of pleasure of Matron's praise in her letter to Thomas – and she'd encountered people she would never have met in little Endstone. She thought of her latest letter from Sanjay Das on the frontline in France; the young Indian soldier she had treated last year wrote to her regularly since he had been discharged and sent back to the battlefields. When would she ever have met someone like him if she had stayed in Endstone?

But the thought of Sanjay gave her a start. How would Jack see her choice to stay in Brighton as anything other than a favouring of her life there over her family, over him? Ellie didn't even think she could convince herself otherwise.

These uncomfortable thoughts nibbled away in her mind, and all the while Maggie's interminable story rattled on, illustrated by elaborate hand gestures, and punctuated by shouts of gusty laughter. Ellie uncrossed and re-crossed her legs pointedly, drained her glass and put it down on the table with unnecessary force. Finally she glared from Jack to Maggie and back again.

When Maggie reached the end of the story at last, Jack laughed – but only politely, Ellie thought smugly – and said, "Anyway, Maggie, I'll see you at the factory tomorrow. I should be taking Ellie home before it gets too late."

Ellie frowned. She was glad that Jack was getting

rid of Maggie, but she didn't feel ready to go home. She had thought they might stay for another drink, spend some more time together, maybe talk a little more about the Endstone job... Not to mention the fact that she hardly required someone to "see her home" when she was perfectly used to going around Brighton all the time on her own.

As they stepped out into the dark square and Jack tucked her hand into his own, she felt grateful for even the ten minutes it would take them to walk back to her house, but at the same time greedy for more.

"Jack!" she said suddenly, tugging on his hand. "Let's not go straight back. Let's go to the cliffs first."

"El," he said with a smile, "it's getting late. I've got work tomorrow."

"Oh, come on. When did you get to be so boring? Just for five minutes, then I'll let you go home for your hot cocoa. I'm only here for a few days. Please!"

He groaned but said, "All right, all right! You'll be the death of me, woman! And we're not going to our hiding place. Just to the top of the cliff there."

"What? Why?"' Their hiding place was a little nook, carved by the elements into the rock beneath an overhang of the cliff. They had visited it together since they were children.

"Ellie! It's pitch black! I for one have no desire to end up broken into pieces on the rocks down there."

"Oh, yes." She laughed. In her excitement she hadn't even thought about that. "All right, then, the clifftop. I'll race you there!"

"El!" Jack's voice drifted up the path from behind her. "What are you doing? You can't see where you're going!"

She felt the adrenaline surging like an electric impulse through her veins. "Jack Scott, are you suggesting for one minute we couldn't both find our way up and down this path blindfolded?" she shouted, the last word coming out in a little yelp as she caught her foot on a fallen branch she hadn't seen in the darkness. She righted herself quickly, but slowed her pace somewhat.

"What was that, Nurse Phillips?" Jack asked in an amused voice, as he drew nearer.

"Nothing, Grandpa," Ellie said, fumbling for his hand. "I just thought I'd wait for you to catch up since you seem nervous about following the path in the dark."

Weaving their fingers together once more, they stepped out of the tree-lined path and into the field that overlooked the cliffs. Little scraps of reflected moonlight flickered on the water and the wind made a hushing sound. Ellie breathed out all the chattering thoughts; breathed in calm and quiet and peace.

The next evening at the train station, Jack twisted his hat between his hands as they waited for the train to arrive.

He blew out a breath. "I just don't understand," he said, for what felt like the twentieth time.

The night before they hadn't talked any more about Thomas's job offer, instead enjoying each other's company, along with the peace on the clifftop. But when he'd arrived at her house after work that afternoon, he'd clearly been thinking about it all day, and just as obviously hadn't heard her tell him that the decision wasn't yet made.

Ellie, in the meantime, felt even more torn. "Jack, I'm not saying I'm not going to take it. You know I'm not saying that! I just need to think a bit more."

"What is there to think about?"

"How can you ask that? You know how good the job in Brighton has been for me!"

"It's the same job here; it's just closer to me! And your family... I thought that would be a good thing."

"It is, of course. But it's not the same job at all – surely you can see that. It will be much slower, much less challenging..."

They both looked up as they heard the rattle of the train's approach. There was a pause, and then Jack said, so softly that Ellie had to strain to hear him over the train's noise, "I just thought you'd want to be here, with me."

Ellie closed her eyes. This was horrible, and it was only getting worse. "You know I want that." She was having almost to shout now. "But I don't want to make any rushed decisions. Please try to understand that."

She opened her eyes and saw that Jack's were fixed on the ground, his pulse visible in his tense jaw.

"Jack, please, I have to go now. Don't be angry with me."

"I'm not. You know I never could be..." But still he didn't look up.

"What rot, you've been angry with me plenty of

times!" Ellie said, trying to make him laugh. She put a hand on his cheek, leaned up and kissed him quickly on the mouth, so that his eyes widened in surprise. "I'll decide soon, Jack, I promise. I'll miss you. I always miss you. Goodbye."

She picked up her bag, opened the carriage door and stepped inside. Then she stood by the window, hands pressed against it, watching until finally, Jack looked up and gave her a wave and a small smile.

FOUR

APRIL

Ellie shook the crisp white sheet out so that it made a snapping noise like a sail in the air and then let it settle down on to the bed. Methodically she began to move around the bed, tucking the sheet in tight to the mattress, but all the while her mind was busy elsewhere.

It had been this way since she had returned from Endstone three weeks previously. Arguments about whether she should stay at the hospital in Brighton or go home to Endstone rolled round and round in her brain; the case for each seemed equally compelling. And so she found herself stuck, unable to move one way or the other, and always ended up abandoning the whole dilemma until another time.

Inevitably, though, the thoughts would come back to bother her in the middle of the night, or when she was eating, or working. She felt as though she got no peace from them.

In the meantime, she had continued writing to Jack as usual – she knew from past experience how dangerous it was to let silence grow between them – but unable to reassure him about her decision, she felt her letters sounded superficial and rambling. His own seemed strangely bland, though she couldn't be sure she wasn't imagining it.

She looked down at the bed she was making and saw that the final corner was creased, the sheet sticking out oddly. Making a noise of exasperation, she untucked it and tried again. Work of this sort didn't help either. This empty ward had to be made ready for a new influx of soldiers, and Ellie had been working alone for hours – cleaning, making up beds, restocking the supply cupboards and trolleys – with no one to distract her and nothing more stimulating to occupy her mind and provide a break from her thoughts.

At that moment, though, the sharp ringing of heels against the floor startled her from her examination of the troublesome corner. She looked up to see the short but solid form of Matron marching briskly towards her, her expression stormy.

"Phillips! A word, please."

"Yes, Matron," Ellie said, her voice coming out whispery in her disquiet.

"Look, Phillips, what's this Doctor Greggs tells me about you being away with the fairies during the surgery on that poor young man's leg yesterday?"

Ellie's mind sprang to life and began to race, her heart thumping painfully. "P–private Harrington?"

"Yes, yes," Matron said impatiently. "The doctor tells me you passed him the scissors to remove a piece of shrapnel when he'd asked for the tweezers. And then you stood there like a post-box when he pointed out the mistake."

"Oh…" All at once Ellie's face as burning as though she had a fever. She had forgotten all about the episode – had barely given it a moment's thought at the time, and certainly not since.

"*Oh?* Is that all you have to say?" Matron's own face

was beginning to colour, her eyebrows inching higher and higher up her forehead. "Apparently it was only the quick response of Nurse Fletcher that prevented disaster."

"Yes," Ellie said. "Yes. I'm . . . I'm sorry."

"Sorry? Phillips, you know well enough at this stage in your nursing work that sorry isn't worth a thing when someone's dying of an infection, or of blood loss. Lord knows you're a dreamer at the best of times, but surgery is *not* the moment for it! I expected better of you!"

"I know. . ."

"Now, as it happens, Doctor Greggs thinks very highly of you, and of course the silly man only mentioned it to me out of concern that there might be something wrong with you that you need help with. . . Is there?"

"Is there. . .?"

"For goodness' sake! Wake up, girl! Is there something the matter with you? Because if there is—"

"No . . . no, Matron." Ellie wrung her hands miserably, wishing she were anywhere other than there. It was all she could do not to turn her back on Matron and run from the room.

"Because he's not the only one to have noticed that you are not up to standard at the moment. Your brain hardly seems to be here at all."

Ellie couldn't hold her gaze any longer. She looked to the floor, though she knew how much it infuriated Matron. Sure enough: "For heaven's sake," Matron went on, her voice getting louder and louder until Ellie cringed, sure that the whole hospital could hear. "You've been in this ward for an hour and still half the beds aren't made! I never thought I'd have to remind *you* that this is not a hobby for you to pass your time – it's a place where very, very sick men come to be healed! You know this! What do you have to say for yourself, young lady?"

What *could* she say? "I'm . . . I'm sorry." Ellie forced herself to lift her chin and look Matron in the eye once more. It was the least she could do. "I'm sorry."

Matron stared back at her for a long moment, then shook her head, turned on her heel, and walked out of the room.

Ellie watched her go, her hands still bunched in the sheet she had been trying so hard to straighten and which was now crumpled beyond all redemption.

Finally, when she was sure that neither the matron, nor anyone else, was about to walk back into the ward, she abandoned her sheet and fled the room. Her feet seemed to fly over the tiles until she reached the staff bathroom. Bursting into a cubicle, she locked the door, put her back to it and slid down until she was sitting on the floor, the tiles cold through her thin dress.

The sobs that tore through her body took her by surprise, both for their violence and for the lack of control she had over them. She couldn't remember crying like this even when her adored father had died, nor when Jack had been away at war, nor when the bomb had fallen on Endstone, injuring and killing people she knew and loved. She lowered her forehead to her knees, allowed herself to wish for a moment that Jack was there with his arms around her, and then abandoned any attempt at restraint. She cried until her throat and eyes were raw, and until there wasn't the breath in her lungs to cry any longer.

Afterwards, she drew herself back upright, washed her face at the sink, returned to the ward and finished her work as quickly and efficiently as she was able. She convinced herself that no one who saw her during the

47

rest of her shift would have known that anything was amiss.

But she had forgotten that her aunt had had a rare day off, and when she walked into their shared room back at the digs that evening, Frances took one look at her face and leapt from the bed, dropping the novel she had been reading. "Ellie! Whatever's the matter? Has something happened?"

All Ellie's hard-won composure vanished and within moments she was sprawled on her aunt's bed, choking out a barely coherent account of the day's events and sobbing into her waist.

"Ellie!" Frances shushed her. "My darling girl! I've never seen you like this in all your life!"

"I know!" Ellie said through a ragged throat. "I . . . the doctor . . . I could have killed that man. . ."

Frances stroked her hair and gave a short laugh. "Ellie, you could not have killed him simply by passing the doctor the scissors instead of the tweezers!"

Ellie opened her mouth to argue but instead a hiccup broke free, stopping her short.

Frances took advantage of this to forge ahead. "Of course, our work is important, and we must try to do our best all the time. And normally that is what you do – what we all do. I think, in truth, one of the things that is upsetting you is the idea that one of the doctors has had anything other than wholehearted praise to offer of you. No, don't disagree with me, Ellie. There's nothing wrong with wanting to do the best job you possibly can, even perhaps being a little competitive about it."

"I've been getting sloppy!" Ellie protested. "And I didn't even realize it! Never mind being competitive! Perhaps I'm not as suited to being a nurse as I believed."

"Nobody who knows you could deny that you've not been yourself of late," Aunt Frances conceded, running a soothing hand over her back. "But that is not the same as not being a good nurse. We all have other things on our mind sometimes. What is bothering you, dear? It might help to talk about it."

Ellie paused, knotting the fabric of her aunt's dress and feeling like a child. She drew a deep breath in, and then let it go. "I think it's about this job that Thomas offered me back in Endstone..."

"Yes?" Aunt Frances said patiently.

"It's just that it keeps playing round and round in my head."

"Well, yes, dear," Frances said, in a tone of absolute forbearance. "I had always imagined you would take it eventually."

Ellie's sat up, her mouth falling open as she looked at her aunt. "But ... but I haven't made up my mind! Not at all! It's driving me tormented trying to make the decision!"

"Ellie," Frances began softly, "it seems to me that your instincts are leading you very clearly in one direction."

"But..." Ellie felt entirely bamboozled. "But which direction is that?"

"Why, back to Endstone, of course."

"But..."

"My poor girl. Do you have any idea how much you've been talking about the place lately? And, perhaps more to the point, about Jack?"

"But – but my work here—"

"Is important – and you have achieved so much. But there will be other volunteer nurses to fill your place here at the hospital, make no mistake. In fact, I believe Matron is expecting a new cohort in the next fortnight. And you will have other chances to continue your learning. I think the Endstone surgery will be a huge opportunity. You will be the only nurse there, and poor Thomas is going to need all the help he can get. In many ways, your responsibilities there will be far greater than they are here."

Ellie wiped her eyes with the back of her hand. "Do you really think so?"

"I'm sure of it," Frances replied.

"You don't think it's me conceding defeat and taking the easy route?"

"Not in the least, you silly thing! And, Ellie, there will be other chances to work in hospitals, and away from Endstone, if that's what you want in the future. You are so young. You have done so much already, but this is only the beginning of your working life. Look, the war is changing everything, but it won't go on for ever. In the meantime, if you think you would be happier being near your family and Jack, then that is where you must be. We have all learnt how important it is to be happy, haven't we?"

Ellie drew a shuddering breath, and realized that all

her counter-arguments had evaporated into thin air. The decision that had seemed completely beyond her for so long was suddenly perfectly clear. "Oh, Aunt Frances..." She fell back into her aunt's arms. "You're completely right! I have been so miserable, and all this time you knew what I needed to do!"

"You silly thing!" Aunt Frances laughed, squeezing her tight. "You knew it too. You were just making things more difficult for yourself."

Ellie joined in with a shaky laugh, sitting up again, and feeling the stresses of the last few weeks almost as a physical sensation as they trickled down her neck and out of her body.

"And just think, Ellie – it was your father's surgery. It feels only right to me that you should be there now, carrying on his work, with his patients, in the town that was his home." Ellie swallowed hard past an uncomfortable knot in her throat and nodded. "I think every day how proud he would be of you, you know," her aunt concluded.

"How do you do that?" Ellie asked her.

"Do what?" Aunt Frances asked, standing up to draw the curtains against the dark sky.

"How do you know exactly the right thing to say and do – all the time?"

"You really *are* a silly thing," Frances said, with another chuckle. "And, by the way, I can read you like a newspaper headline. Now," she went on, as Ellie gave her a mock scowl, "go and wash your face, and let's have some supper."

"All right."

"And then I imagine you might have some letters you'll be wanting to write."

Ellie drew out her handkerchief and blew her nose before answering: "I will?"

"Well, yes," Frances replied with an air of studied casualness. "You'll be wanting to write to Thomas ... and your mother ... and perhaps to a certain young Master Scott..."

Ellie grinned as Frances swept from the room, calling, "I'll put the kettle on! You can make a start on those letters now, if you'd like..."

Ellie leapt to her feet and hurried to the writing bureau in the corner of the room. But as she drew out a fresh sheet of paper, she decided that, while she would write to Thomas and let him know that she would be taking up his kind offer, she wanted to surprise her mother and Charlie – yes, and Jack – and give them the news face-to-face.

Imagining Jack's expression when she told him, she abandoned her writing and collapsed backwards on the bed. She knew it had hurt him that she hadn't made the decision straight away, but she was sure of how happy he would be now. He would laugh at her, she thought wryly, for the fact that once again she had taken so long to make the decision that had been so clear to everybody else. She pulled a pillow into her chest and hugged it tightly. On this occasion, she didn't care how much he laughed at her. She just couldn't wait to see him.

FIVE

MAY

It was strange walking up the garden path once again, her big suitcase knocking against her knee. In some ways it felt like no time at all since she had last been here; in others it couldn't have felt more different from her last visit. Everything had changed.

Once again the garden was looking very overgrown, though now at least it was crocuses, bluebells, lilacs and peonies that were fighting their way through the wild grass and weeds. She would have to get it back in shape now she was home, Ellie thought. She could resurrect her mother's long-neglected vegetable patches, too: grow some potatoes and cabbages, maybe some beans.

It had been sad saying goodbye to everyone at the hospital – especially Grace, some of her longer-term patients, and Matron. Ellie laughed to think of the latter. She would never have imagined when she first met the formidable matron that she would come to feel such respect and even affection for her.

As soon as she had made the decision to return to Endstone, Ellie's concentration levels, and therefore her work, had returned to normal. Matron had been very supportive of the decision and had told Ellie that Thomas would be "lucky to have her" in the surgery. The thought had been making Ellie beam ever since. So too had the fact that, as she was leaving, Grace had tugged her into a quiet corner to brandish the pretty solitaire ring on her finger. "Private Lessing..." was all she managed to get out, but that had been enough to fill Ellie with happiness that felt like bubbles in her throat.

Perhaps more than anything, Ellie would miss her aunt. She had always been close to her Aunt Frances, had admired and wanted to be like her since she was a very young girl. But over the last eighteen or so months living and working together, they had become true friends. As soon as this wretched war was over, Ellie would make sure she got to Brighton regularly to visit her, of that she was determined.

Dropping her bag at the front door, Ellie peeped through the window into the kitchen. The sight that greeted her made her heart squeeze tight. Mother and Charlie were sitting at the table, boiled eggs and salad before them. Mother's posture was strangely hunched, a grey shawl drawn tightly around her narrow shoulders. Charlie kept up a constant stream of conversation – Ellie could hear his piping voice in snatches through the window – but the best Mother managed was the occasional wan smile in his direction.

Ellie paused for a moment, watching them, but then knocked decisively on the window. Her mother's startled expression – eyes and mouth so wide – made her wonder briefly if she ought to have warned her she was coming after all, but then Charlie caught sight of her and dimples appeared in his round cheeks.

"Ellie!"

She smiled and waved, before walking to the front door. By the time she opened it, Charlie was struggling down the hallway with a chair, clearly ready to do the job himself.

"Ellie!" he exclaimed again, wrapping his arms around her waist.

Mother appeared in the doorway looking so frail and bewildered that Ellie briefly felt the urge to cry. "Eleanor? We weren't expecting you, were we? Perhaps a letter went astray..."

"No, Mother," Ellie said with a small smile, staggering over to her with Charlie hanging like an anchor around her middle. "No, I thought I'd make it a surprise this time. You see, I won't be visiting again for a while."

Mother's face sagged. "Oh..."

Ellie hurried to put her out of her misery. "No, it's just that I won't be going back to Brighton this time... I'm staying!"

Mother's expression remained blank. "You're ... staying?" she repeated slowly, her forehead creased.

"Yes, Mother," Ellie replied patiently. "Thomas has offered me a job in the surgery. I'm staying here, in Endstone."

"You're staying..." Mother said again. The furrows

on her brow eased. "You're staying." She shook herself. "That's ... that's *wonderful* news, Ellie." Her eyes looked damp as Ellie, again feeling in danger of tears herself, leaned forwards to give her a kiss on the cheek.

"You staying here, Ellie?" Charlie asked, swinging from her waist and causing her tired muscles to protest.

"Oof! I am, Charlie boy. And you're going to help me get the garden shipshape for growing our own food, now that you're such a big boy."

"Hmm," Charlie said dubiously.

After lunch, Ellie set her mother up in the back garden with a cup of tea by her side and a blanket over her knees. She was concerned by Mother's greyish complexion and convinced that some fresh air and spring sunshine would help.

This done, she cleaned up the lunch things, then set herself to getting the house back into some kind of order. She swept, mopped and dusted in every room – thinking of the floors in her ward that she had kept spotless at all times – and opened the windows wide to let out the fusty, stale air. Then she stripped all the beds and heaved the sheets out to the big laundry basin.

All the while, Charlie danced around her legs, singing a little song of his own invention and begging for Ellie to take him to the beach. At first Ellie had smiled, scooping him out of the way and attempting to give him little tasks to do to help her. But when he jumped on her back so that she staggered forward, plunging her arms deep into the cold water in the laundry basin, and on going inside to find something dry to wear, discovered his muddy footprints all over her newly clean floor, she snapped.

"Charlie! Look at this floor! That's very naughty of you. You can fetch the broom and mop and clean it while I get a dry blouse to put on."

"No!" Charlie crowed from the doorway.

"*Not* 'no'," Ellie countered. "Do it at once, please."

"Eleanor!" Mother's plaintive voice sounded from the other end of the corridor, where she had emerged from the back garden. "Is all the shouting really necessary? And you can hardly expect Charlie to help with the housework!"

Ellie felt her teeth clench together. A thousand

retorts sprang to her lips but she kept them tightly closed. There was no point. Her relationship with her mother might have improved hugely in recent times, but Mother still wouldn't see her as an adult in the household; she certainly would never concede that her son should participate in tasks around the house.

It didn't matter, Ellie told herself fiercely, changing her blouse upstairs in the room she shared with Charlie. Mother was scarcely aware of what happened around her these days, she was so locked into her world of headaches and tiredness. Ellie was back now, and she would get things in order around here – including making sure Charlie did not grow to expect his mother and sister to wait on him.

Still, as Ellie looked around the little room, so familiar in its childishness, unchanged since she had been as small as Charlie, she felt a wave of panic. Suddenly, briefly, it was as though Brighton had all been a dream; as though working in the factory had been a dream; it was as though she was right back where she had been when Mother had insisted she give up school and stay home to help around the house instead, and that nothing at all had changed.

Bracing her hands against the top of the chest of drawers, she took some deep, calming breaths. It wasn't true. Even if everything else had been the same, *she* was different. She had seen and done and learned so much; met people unlike any she had ever encountered in Endstone. Those things couldn't be undone. She could never go back to the way she had been. And, anyway, she told herself firmly as she walked back down the stairs, Jack would be so pleased when he found out she was back for good – that alone would make it all worthwhile.

She felt better later that afternoon, when she went to visit Thomas in the surgery. Things certainly seemed to have become rather chaotic there, and Ellie immediately began to plan how she might organize them better. Over a pot of tea, Thomas went through the list of patients needing regular visits, and outlined which ones he had thought he might allocate to Ellie's care.

"I thought we might go together to visit Mr Harris on his farm this afternoon," Thomas said. "Do you remember him?"

"I think so," Ellie replied. "He used to come into

the village some evenings after his work was done for the day, didn't he?"

"That's right. The poor man had to have a leg amputated following an injury, and I've been treating his other foot for trench foot leading to gangrene. You'll need to visit him regularly to make sure he's keeping it clean, and that the amputation site is healing well."

"All right," Ellie replied, nodding. This type of injury was all too familiar to her after her work in the Brighton hospital.

"You have your bicycle with you, don't you? His farm is a few miles out of town."

They cycled alongside each other at a companionable pace, following the main road out of the town and into the countryside.

"I'm so glad to have you here, Ellie," Thomas said, as they passed the turn-off for the train station. "You will be such a help. And I will pay you a decent wage; hopefully that will assist with lessening the blow of leaving Brighton." He glanced over and gave her a small smile.

Ellie smiled back. She had scarcely thought about the financial side of things among all her other considerations. But there was no question that it would make things easier at home if she were earning a proper salary. As a volunteer nurse in Brighton, she had only been given a small allowance intended to cover her expenses. She had sent every penny that she could spare home to her mother, knowing – despite Mother's aversion to talking about it – that things were very tight following Father's death.

"Thank you, Thomas," she said. "I'm glad to be working with you too."

After another ten minutes or so, they reached a gate through which Ellie could see a rough driveway leading to a small farmhouse.

"Mr Harris used to be predominantly a cattle farmer," Thomas said softly as they dismounted and began to push their bicycles down the track. "He and his brother-in-law took over the running of the farm after his parents died. But he sold his herd when the two of them went away to war – and just as well since he wouldn't be able to manage them now. His sister helps keep things going with a small number of crops – but it's a struggle on top of taking care of her husband and the children."

They leaned their bicycles against the front of the house, and Thomas knocked loudly on the door, before entering.

"Good afternoon, Mr Harris!" he called brightly. "It's Dr Pritchard!"

A voice greeted them from the kitchen, and they walked in. Ellie glanced around at the closed curtains and dusty surfaces.

"Hello," said a figure from the kitchen table.

Ellie squinted through the gloom. She remembered Mr Harris as a big man, but he looked hollowed out now, like a toy bear with the stuffing removed. His blue eyes seemed more dull, though the skin around them still crinkled as Thomas introduced her.

"You remember Eleanor Phillips, don't you?"

"Indeed I do – Dr Phillips' daughter," Mr Harris replied. "He was a great man, Miss Phillips – the village is the poorer without him."

"Thank you, sir. It's kind of you to say so."

"Ellie's following in her father's footsteps," Thomas went on, "as a nurse. And she's going to be calling in to check on you."

"That's good of you, dear. I'm rather a pathetic

specimen these days, and I could do with the help – not to mention the company!"

Ellie couldn't keep her eyes from running over the cluttered surfaces, the pile of crockery in the sink.

"My sister does what she can," Mr Harris said apologetically, following the direction of her gaze. "But she has a job on taking care of the farm with only some other veterans and my young nephews to help. My mother always said I should get myself a nice wife," he continued, with a brief laugh, "but I suppose I wouldn't be much of a husband to anyone now. It never occurred to me that I might not be able to look after myself one day." Ellie winced at the bitterness in his voice; at the thought of his isolation and despair.

She and Thomas checked on Mr Harris's injuries and tidied things up in the house a little. Before leaving, Ellie promised she would be back to see him again in a few days.

As they collected their bicycles from the front of the house, Ellie looked at her watch. It was after six. Jack would be home from work by now!

They cycled back at a brisk pace and when they reached the village, she bid Thomas goodbye, turning right across the square instead of left for home. She pedalled furiously, the juddering of her wheels over the cobbles making her teeth rattle.

Arriving on Jack's street, she freewheeled the last couple of metres, before dropping her feet down to come to an abrupt halt outside his house. She could see that the front door was ajar, so she leaned her bicycle as gently as she could against the wall, pushed the door wider and tiptoed down the narrow hallway in the direction of the kitchen. But the sound of raised voices made her stop short.

"...eighteen next month, Mam."

"I know that, Jack, but I don't see why you're in such a hurry to get on the list. If you just keep quiet, I'm sure it'll take them a while to get round to calling you up – and who knows? The war might have ended by then."

Ellie felt bile rising in her throat and her head began to pound.

"You can't really believe that, Mam," Jack was saying. "Not after all this time..."

Suddenly the surprise didn't seem such a good idea. Ellie retreated back down the hallway, then hesitated before knocking loudly on the front door. This time she walked much more slowly in the direction of the kitchen. By the time she stepped through the doorway, Jack and his mother were on their feet, their chairs pushed back from the table.

"Ellie!" Mabel exclaimed. "I didn't know you were due a visit." She glanced questioningly at Jack.

"Nor did I," was all he said.

Ellie frowned. He didn't look pleased, as she had imagined he would. Over and over she had imagined it. He just looked confused. "It's not a visit," she said. "I'm here to stay. I'm back."

Mabel seemed to understand first. "That's wonderful, Ellie!" she exclaimed.

"You accepted the job..." Jack said slowly.

"Yes," Ellie replied, her voice sounding flat even to her own ears.

"Well," Jack said. He grinned but there was no real joy in it. "Well, good – I was beginning to think Thomas might have given it to someone else with all the time you were taking to make your mind up."

Ellie stared back at him, searching his face for something – though she couldn't have said what, exactly.

"Jack!" His mother admonished him. "Don't be sulky – you're too old for such nonsense! What does it matter how long Ellie took to decide? She's here now, and we're all very glad to have her back."

"Of course we are," Jack said, and at last he opened his arms. Ellie stepped into them awkwardly. "Of course we are."

SIX

A few days later, Ellie and Jack finally had some time alone together. It had been difficult to snatch more than a few moments between their respective jobs and helping out with their families. With his father still in prison following the explosion at the old factory, and his older brother, Will, away at war, Jack's mother leaned on him for support almost as much as Ellie's did on her.

They were sitting in their favourite clearing in the woods on the edge of Endstone. It was the warmest day of the year so far and late spring was in evidence all around them. Wildflowers bloomed in confetti-like clusters about the old oak tree, bees humming fuzzily between them. Sparrows darted to and fro in the branches of the tree and the sound of the river burbled in the background.

Ellie was glad to be on her own with Jack, and relieved that he was behaving a little more like his usual self. She hadn't told him about overhearing his conversation with Mabel; in fact she had been trying to think about it as little as possible. Her head was in his lap and he poked bits of leaves and flowers into her hair while she chattered about her new work with the patients of Endstone, desperate not to allow any trace of that strangeness to creep back into their conversation.

"Poor Mr Harris," she was concluding. "It occurs to me when I go round there that speaking to me might be the first time he's had any reason to use his voice that day – if his sister hasn't been round, I mean. And sometimes when I'm about to leave it seems as though he's finding any excuse to keep me talking, to keep me there, just so that he's not on his own."

"Poor chap," Jack said with a sigh, pushing a last daisy stem into the tangle of hair by her right ear. "That's sad."

"I know." She pushed herself up to sitting, sending

leaves and petals tumbling from her hair to the ground. "I think he might be the loneliest person I've ever met. Aside from Mother, of course."

"Perhaps you should introduce them," Jack said with a half smile as Ellie stood up, brushing down her skirt.

"Hmmm, misery loves company; is that the idea?" She held out her hand to help him to his feet. "I'm not sure my mother loves any sort of company."

"Now, now," Jack said, lacing his fingers through hers, swinging their hands back and forth as they began to walk back towards the village. "She's better than she used to be."

"That's true. She doesn't even mind *your* company these days," Ellie said with a grin, earning herself a shove in the direction of a muddy ditch.

They fell into silence as they walked on. After so many years of friendship, Ellie was usually perfectly comfortable being with Jack and not talking, but today it felt as though they were both tiptoeing around the perimeter of so many things they couldn't speak about. It made the short distance to the gate at the edge of the village feel much further than usual, but eventually they emerged through it, walking together into the sun-dappled square.

Ellie heard the clattering footsteps just a second before she felt a solid weight ram into Jack, knocking him forwards and forcing their hands apart.

"Oof!"

"Ha! There you are, Jack!"

Ellie felt almost winded by the physical shock, a sensation that was not eased when she realized that the new arrival was Maggie – the girl from the pub that day back in February.

"Oh, hello, Maggie!" Jack said with a surprised laugh.

"I've been looking for you all over," she said, leaning in towards him. Once again it seemed as though she hadn't noticed Ellie at all.

"Have you?" Jack replied, grinning. "Well, now you've found me."

Ellie couldn't help herself. "Do you usually interrupt people's private conversations so rudely?" She cut across, drawing Maggie's attention to her at last, while wincing internally at how posh and cold her voice sounded, especially in contrast to Maggie's down-to-earth tones.

"Ellie!" Jack scowled at her. She felt her cheeks flame, but kept her chin lifted defiantly.

Maggie looked taken aback, but only for a matter of seconds. Then she grinned. "Yeah, I suppose I probably do. I'm not known for my refined ways! Sorry to be so *rude*. I'll leave you both to it. See you around, Jack."

Jack gave her an apologetic wave as she sauntered off across the square, then rounded on Ellie.

"I'm sorry!" she said hurriedly, trying to pre-empt his irritation. "But you have to admit, she *was* rude!"

"So were you! What on earth's got into you? She was only being friendly."

"To you, maybe. She doesn't like me any more than I do her."

"You're being silly. What reason do you have not to like her? Or to think she doesn't like you? And how could she have interrupted us anyway? We weren't even talking!"

"I know, Jack!" Ellie exploded, making him widen his eyes and take a half step backwards. "*Why* aren't you talking to me? What are you hiding from me?"

"Hiding?" His eyebrows crept higher and his hands

opened in a gesture of supplication. "Ellie, I honestly don't know what you're on about."

She closed her eyes briefly and took a slow breath. When she next spoke, her voice sounded calmer, more under control. "I'm sorry. I'm sorry, all right? I didn't mean to be rude or silly. I think I just..." She trailed off, then collected herself. "Look, I heard you speaking to your mum the other day ... about joining up again..."

His expression had been blank with confusion, but now his eyes narrowed slightly. "Eavesdropping, were we? That's not nice, Ellie."

"I didn't mean to!" she said indignantly. "It wasn't on purpose! I didn't knock at the front door because I wanted to surprise you – not that you seemed at all pleased to see me – and you weren't exactly speaking quietly."

Jack was chewing on the inside of his cheek, fidgeting on his feet. "So what is it I'm in trouble for, El? Not making enough fuss of you when you came back, or talking about joining up again? Maybe talking too loudly—"

"Both—" She broke off as he gave a short, humourless laugh. "No, no, that's not what I mean.

You're not in trouble at all. I'm simply trying to explain why I'm upset. I've only just got back here, and now you're planning to go away and put yourself in the most terrible danger. And you weren't even going to tell me..."

"Ellie," Jack said wearily, rubbing a hand over his face, "why are you acting as though I have any say in this? You know very well I'll be eighteen in a few weeks, and then I'll be called up just the same as all the other lads, whatever I do. I'm sorry you had to hear me talking like that, but we've all known this was coming."

"But why would you hurry it along? It's like your mum said, if you lie low and keep quiet about it, maybe by the time they get round to calling you up the war will be over..."

"Lie low like a coward while other blokes do my duty?" Jack said coldly. "Hide at home with the children, the women, the invalids, when I'm perfectly able to go and fight. Is that what you're suggesting I do?

"It's not being cowardly, Jack! You've seen for yourself how much you risk being out there. And *I've* seen the men that come back – or at least what's left of them."

He flinched. "The risks are just the same for everyone, Ellie. Why should I be spared them? And you're right, I have seen how bloody awful it is for myself. I don't need you reminding me when I've no choice in whether I go."

Ellie fell silent for a moment, feeling her chest heaving with her laboured breath. She became aware for the first time of the sounds in the square around them – footsteps over the cobbles, murmured conversation, the distant crashing of waves over at Big Beach – and of people looking in their direction.

Who cares? she thought to herself. *This is too important to worry about what other people think.* But she was clearly getting nowhere in this line of argument with Jack. It was as though they were speaking different languages, they were so far from being able to understand each other's perspective.

"Fine," she said at last. "If you won't think about the danger to yourself, then what about your responsibilities here? Mabel and Anna and George need you with your father and Will both away. *I* need you! I've come all the way back from Brighton, given up a job that I loved, to be with you. And now you're leaving?"

"Never mind silly – you're being ridiculous, Ellie!"
Jack said, no longer trying to hide his frustration.
"There's nothing I can do about my responsibilities at
home – pretty much every other man in the country is in
the same position! And don't try to make me feel guilty
about you leaving Brighton. You took long enough to
make that decision – and you'd never have done it if it
didn't suit yourself!"

"That's not fair!" she cried, knowing that she
sounded like a child, but unable to stop herself. "I came
back because of my *own* responsibilities – to my family,
to you! And now I find all you seem to want to do is run
around with this Maggie character, while planning to
go away and leave me all over again. No doubt *Maggie*
thinks you're a real hero, running off to war."

Jack rolled his eyes. Ellie dug her nails into her palms
in irritation at the dismissive gesture. "You know what,
Ellie, why don't you let me know once you've settled
on what it is you're annoyed with me for, so I've some
hope of defending myself? Stop bringing Maggie into
this – it has nothing to do with her. Yes, she's my friend.
She's been a good one too: someone to talk to, keeping
me company while you've been away, so engrossed in

your life in Brighton. Can you blame me for wanting a friend who was actually around, who was happy to spend time with me?"

Ellie's stomach plummeted as though she'd gone over a sudden hill on her bicycle. "Jack!"

"And if you must know, yes, she has been a lot more supportive about me joining up."

"She knows?" Ellie's voice sounded husky now. "She knows all about it, and you hadn't even told me?"

They both fell silent again, staring at each other.

At last, shaking his head and puffing his breath out, Jack looked away. "I think we should probably leave it for today, don't you?" he said, his voice softer. "We don't seem to be getting anywhere with this conversation."

"No . . . I mean, yes, let's leave it," she replied stiffly.

"I'm sorry if I upset you." He still wouldn't meet her eye.

"Me too."

"All right." He leaned over and kissed her briefly on the forehead, before turning away. "I'll see you, Ellie."

"Goodbye..."

She watched him walk away, before she turned

and ran across the square towards Big Beach, her eyes burning and her jaw clenched tight. Reaching the beach, she stumbled towards where the grey foaming water met the sand, checked to make sure no one was around, then screamed and screamed into the pounding waves until her voice ran out and her throat was raw.

SEVEN

JUNE

It was early morning, and Ellie was getting ready to go out to work for the day. She had taken her mother a cup of tea but left Charlie sleeping in their room. As she piled things into her bag with one hand, she gnawed at the nails of the other, which were ragged by now. She and Jack hadn't spoken since that horrible row a couple of weeks previously. But today was his birthday – he was eighteen – and it felt so wrong not to have any plans to see him; not to know if she would even be welcome if she turned up at his house later on.

She gasped as she tore at a hangnail, making it bleed,

but at least finally shaking herself out of her stupor. Forcing her bag closed, she marched out of the front door, shutting it softly behind her so as not to wake Charlie. The longer he stayed asleep, the easier Mother's day would be.

As Ellie turned, she saw Jack standing at the end of the path, and at once she felt a broad smile spread across her face and her shoulders seemed to release away from her ears. "Jack!" She ran down the path and into his arms, wrapping her own around him. "Happy birthday. I'm so pleased you came."

He ran a hand up and down her back and kissed the top of her head, but his voice sounded nervous as he said, "Thanks, El. Me too."

She looked up at him questioningly, his tone catching her attention immediately.

"I..." he went on hesitantly. "Well, I wanted to see you anyway. But came early because I thought I should tell you... I didn't want you hearing it from anyone else..."

There was a rushing noise in her ears. "What? Tell me, Jack. Tell me quickly."

"I'm going to catch the train to Canterbury today, to

join up. I know you won't be happy about it, but I hope you can understand my reasons, at least."

She took a step back, trying to keep her voice level. "So nothing I said the other day made the slightest bit of difference? Your mind is completely made up and I get no say in the matter?"

He sighed. "On this occasion, no, you don't, Ellie. Nor do I. None of us has any choice in this. That's war, isn't it? I'm not sure what it is you expect me to do differently. Do you want me to become a conscientious objector or something?"

Ellie paused. In truth she hadn't thought about what he would do if he didn't sign up now he was eighteen – she hadn't really allowed herself to, since she knew in her heart that he always would. But now that he said it... "Why not?"

"I can't do that."

"You *won't*."

"Ellie..."

"Just go, Jack," she said, past a lump in her throat. "There's clearly nothing I can say to change your mind, so I don't think I can bear to look at you any more."

His shoulders dropped. "Right. Well, thanks for

your support, Ellie." He turned and walked down the path to collect his bicycle, and before she knew it he was gone.

Ellie scrubbed furiously at her eyes, then went to fetch her own bicycle. Work. That was the only thing that would keep her mind from this horrible situation.

It was a busy day of cycling round from patient to patient, and it did help to keep her mind occupied. So many people were suffering so much, and it was rewarding to be able to make things easier for them in any small way.

But by three o'clock she had finished her rounds for the day, and she felt the uncomfortable thoughts creeping back in. She remembered that she needed to take her family's ration books to the village store to collect some of the groceries they were running low on at home, so turned her bicycle from the terraced streets behind the square, where she had been visiting her last patient of the day, and headed back towards the centre.

She leaned her bicycle against the front of the shop – the large plate-glass window had been replaced following the bomb explosion the previous year – and then paused. Perhaps visiting the shop run by his family was not the best idea when she was trying so hard not to think about Jack. Still, the shopping was needed, and when she had it she could go home and distract herself by looking after Mother and Charlie. She pushed the door open decisively, making the bell jangle with reassuring familiarity.

Jack's sister, Anna, was serving customers behind the counter, and Ellie could see his mother moving around in the back, filling jars from big hessian sacks. In one of Jack's letters when she was still in Brighton he had told her that before rationing had been introduced, the food shortages had led to huge queues snaking out of the shop and round the square. Ellie had seen similar scenes in Brighton. Now, there were just three or four women waiting to be served; things appeared to be calmer.

Ellie responded to Anna's wave, and then joined the back of the queue, glancing at the newspaper headlines on the rack while she waited. At last she reached the front and exchanged greetings with Anna. Jack's sister had been badly affected by the bomb explosion the previous year, not least because her little brother

George had been seriously hurt, but by now she seemed to have mostly returned to her normal mischievous self.

While she weighed out Ellie's cheese and butter, she said, with a cheeky smile, "I hear you've met our Jack's new friend, Maggie Brown."

Ellie made a noncommittal noise, but instantly started chewing on a nail again.

"Quite something, isn't she?" Anna said with a laugh, pushing her thick copper braid back over her shoulder. "She's Rosemary Wicker's cousin, did you know that?" Ellie shook her head, not trusting herself to speak. "Yeah, that's why she and her mum moved here after Rosemary's dad went missing in action. They all live together on Charles Street."

Something more than a "hmmm" seemed required so Ellie said, "I see."

"I'll tell you something," Anna went on, wrapping up the cheese in greaseproof paper. "Since the moment she arrived in town, that girl has had her eye on our Jack. A right shine she's taken to him."

Ellie tried to look unbothered but she was becoming more and more anxious to get out of the shop. Anna was still grinning, seemingly unaware of Ellie's discomfort. "I'd keep an eye on her if I were you. I know you and Jack have always been best mates, or whatever it is you are" – Ellie felt her cheeks beginning to burn – "but that Maggie seems like a girl who gets what she wants. And she's clearly decided she wants Jack. Who knows why…"

Ellie had had enough. She slammed her hands down on the counter, making Anna jump.

"Well, it's just as well Jack's off to war again, then, isn't it – and that he'll no doubt get himself killed. So we won't have to worry about who he chooses to spend his time with, will we?"

"What?" The change to Anna's face was instant. The smile disappeared as though it had never been there, and the colour drained suddenly, making her freckles stand out more sharply than ever.

Oh, God. "I…" Ellie began helplessly.

Mabel walked out hurriedly from the back room, having overheard the last part of the conversation. She put an arm around Anna. "I was going to tell you, love, I just…" Her voice cracked and Anna turned into her embrace.

"Already?"

"I'm sorry," Ellie said. "I thought you knew."

But the two Scott women were lost in their own despair, and seemed hardly to hear her. Leaving her coupons and coins on the counter, Ellie seized her shopping and ran from the shop.

That evening, she was just finishing clearing away the supper things when, through the kitchen window, she saw Jack approaching on his bicycle once more. She let the plate she had been washing fall back into the sink with a clatter, yanked the back door open and ran out into the garden.

She waited, leaning against the wall of the house, breathing heavily and feeling rather ridiculous. But she couldn't bear the thought of seeing Jack now; couldn't even imagine what she would say to him. All afternoon she had tormented herself with thoughts of him and Maggie. Maybe Maggie was the real reason he hadn't been as happy to have her home as she had imagined he would be. Maybe Ellie had left him alone for too long, and now she had lost him completely. She knew she had neglected him when she first moved to Brighton. If she was honest, there had even been a time last year when she had thought she might be developing feelings beyond friendship for Sanjay, the young Indian soldier she had treated at the hospital. Perhaps it wasn't fair to blame Jack if he had fallen for someone else. She glanced down at where her chewed nails had gouged angry red crescents into her palms and gave a short, bitter laugh. Not blaming him would require further effort.

"Eleanor? Eleanor?" Her mother's voice drifted into the garden from the hallway.

Ellie ducked lower in case her mother walked into the back room and saw her through the window.

"Eleanor?" She heard the murmur of voices and, keeping low, tiptoed to stand by the back door. The voices were clearer now.

"...to worry," Jack was saying. "I just wanted to tell her... Well, she knows I went to Canterbury to sign up today. Anyway, it seems they want me sooner than I'd thought for training. Right away, in fact." Ellie's stomach churned queasily. "I'm to report to the training camp in Folkestone tomorrow morning."

"Oh..." Mother began awkwardly. "Well, I'll tell her as soon as I see her. I can't think where she's got to; she was just here."

"Thank you, Mrs Phillips," Jack replied smoothly. "I'll be at home with my family this evening. If you could possibly tell her that too."

"I will." There was another brief silence. "Well, good luck, Jack. You will be missed here."

Ellie felt a hot tear spill from her eyelid and tumble down her face.

"Thank you," Jack said again. "I will miss everyone too. But I'll be training in Folkestone for the first few months at least, so hopefully I'll be able to get home every so often. At least before I ship out. Say cheerio to Charlie for me too."

"I could fetch him now?" Mother offered.

"No, no – thank you. But it's probably hard for the little chap to understand, and I don't want to get him all wound up right before his bedtime."

"You're probably right. Well, take care of yourself. I do mean that. There are a lot of people here who will be waiting for your safe return."

"I will, Mrs Phillips."

As they said their goodbyes, Ellie sank down on to her haunches, her back against the wall. She lowered her head to her knees, pressing them against her aching eye sockets. He was going. He was really going.

She wasn't sure how long it was after he left that she finally felt able to stand, hoping that her face didn't look too ravaged. The light had taken on a dusky quality. Realizing that she would need an excuse for her absence, she seized the laundry basket from by the door, and pulled the washing down from the line, not caring that some of it wasn't completely dry. Taking one last deep breath, and using the back of a hand to wipe at her face, she walked through the door back into the kitchen.

Mother was still sitting at the table, staring at her hands. She jumped when Ellie appeared. "There you are!" she said. "Where have you been?"

Ellie gestured at the laundry basket, not daring to speak yet.

Mother looked pointedly out of the window at the dwindling light and then shook her head. "Well, you missed Jack. I'm surprised you didn't hear him if you were in the garden – that boy has always had the loudest voice. He's lucky Charlie didn't realize he was here too, or he'd never have got away... Anyway, it would seem his training for the army begins tomorrow, in

Folkestone. You should get round to see him tonight if you want to say goodbye."

Ellie just shrugged, unfolding the ironing board and setting the iron to heat on the stove.

Mother looked at her through narrowed eyes. "What on earth is going on with you? Isn't it his birthday today too? I'm sure in the past I would have had to drag you away from him to do your chores."

"Well, that was in the past," Ellie said with a sniff as she stretched a sheet across the ironing board. "I am not a child any more, Mother."

"Hmmm. Well, be that as it may, you should go and see him this evening. Who knows how easy it will be for him to get home once his training starts."

Ellie made a noise in the back of her throat that could have meant anything, or nothing at all, and began sweeping the iron across the sheet.

"Eleanor..."

"First I need to get Charlie ready for bed."

"And when are you going to do that, given that you've just started ironing?"

Ellie looked at the iron in her hand as though surprised to find it there.

"Oh, never mind. It's a most peculiar time to be starting laundry, anyway," Mother said. "I'll finish that sheet and you can go and look after Charlie."

Before her mother could give her any more knowing looks, Ellie hurried from the room to find her little brother, who was playing upstairs.

"Come on, Charlie, bedtime," she said.

He grumbled as she tugged off his grubby clothes, keeping one fist tight around his toy train, which made the whole process much more difficult.

"Charlie!"

"Where's Jack?" he asked as she tried to force the train and hand through his pyjama sleeve.

"Would you just... Oof! For goodness' sake. Can you at least hold it in your other hand while I do this?"

He swapped the train to his other hand but insisted: "Where's *Jack*?"

"He's not here."

"But where *is* he?"

"At his own house, Charlie. He doesn't live here, you know."

"Can I see him?"

"No." She stood him up to put his pyjama bottoms on.

"Why?"

"Because it's your bedtime and he's not here. And," she went on hurriedly before he could ask why again, "you should get used to it because he's going away, so we won't be seeing him for a while." *Or ever again*, she thought to herself grimly.

Charlie looked stricken. He kept one foot firmly on the floor so she couldn't lift it into his pyjama leg. "But *why*?"

"Ugh. Because he's a very silly boy. Like someone else I could mention. Lift your foot!"

"But *why*?"

"Charlie!" Her voice came out almost as a roar. "Stop asking me daft questions and get into your pyjamas, or you can get yourself ready for bed from now on."

Charlie's mouth snapped shut in surprise, before opening wide again in a wail.

"What on earth is going on in here?" Mother had appeared at the door. Charlie, still making a sound like the squeal of a train whistle, ran to her and hid his face against her hip. "Eleanor?"

"He's ... he's being..." Ellie trailed off, feeling as

though she could happily cry and demand comfort herself.

"A child?" Mother suggested. "Well, it seems he's not the only one, despite you telling me only moments ago that you're an adult now. I think you'd better go to bed before you cause any more upset, don't you?"

Ellie nodded miserably and went to get into her nightgown.

Half an hour later, she was lying staring at the dark ceiling, feeling as though she would never get to sleep, imagining Jack, spending his last night in his own bed. Was he disappointed that she hadn't come round? Maybe he had been secretly relieved. Perhaps he had gone for a drink with Maggie in the Dog and Duck instead.

She turned angrily on to her side, pulling the blanket with her, and then jumped. Charlie's face, pale in the darkness, stared back at her. He stood by her bed, clutching his teddy. "Ellie? You 'right, Ellie?"

She smiled and pulled back the blanket, making a space for him. "I'm all right, Charlie. Come on in, then."

He clambered up next to her, reaching up and

knotting his fingers into her hair. She pulled his warm, solid form close and rested her chin on his head. At last, feeling the reassuring thud of his heartbeat against her ribs, she drifted off to sleep.

EIGHT

JULY

Ellie finished removing the last of the stitches from Private Joseph's head wound, dabbing at the slightly puckered skin across the back of his scalp with a damp cloth.

"This is healing really nicely, Christopher," she said to the top of his dark head. "I don't think the scar will be at all noticeable once the hair grows back. Whoever did these sutures at the base hospital in France did a good job."

The young soldier nodded, but otherwise didn't respond. In truth, Ellie was far more concerned by his other symptoms: his trembling hands, unfocused eyes that frequently filled with tears, his gaunt frame. He and Ellie had been at school together, he a few years ahead of her. He had played football with Jack and had always been kind to Charlie. But they might as well have been complete strangers for all the recognition he showed her now.

Ellie sat down to face him again. They were in the examination room at the surgery, where, in what felt like a different lifetime, Ellie had helped her father to organize the patients' files. Thomas was out visiting Stephen Chase, yet another young soldier who had been treated for pneumonia in one of the London hospitals, and now had been sent home for the last stage of his recovery.

"How are you feeling otherwise, Christopher?" she asked. "Any dizziness or lack of appetite?"

He shook his head, still not meeting her gaze.

"Have you noticed any improvement in the vision in your right eye?" In addition to the head injury, the private had suffered a shrapnel wound to his eye that had left him partially blind.

Again he shook his head.

"I'm sure your mother is taking good care of you,"

she tried now. "You always were her golden boy, weren't you?"

He lifted his head and looked at her blankly.

"But you must make sure you're getting enough to eat. I know it's tricky with rationing, but we've no shortage of potatoes, and that's just the sort of thing you need to be eating plenty of to build your strength up again."

"What for?" he said at last, his voice scratchy and scarcely above a whisper, but with a fierceness to it that took her by surprise. "So I can be sent back out there?"

"No," Ellie said at once, reaching forward and taking his hand. "No, absolutely not. With your loss of sight, there's no question of that. But we all have to find a way to go on, Christopher, to somehow get on with life. And at the moment I'm worried a sharp gust of wind from Big Beach could carry you off." She smiled but he was still staring fixedly at their joined hands.

"How can I..." He stopped, screwed his eyes tightly closed and then started again. "How can I ... get on with life, as you say, when the other chaps... When they're..."

Ellie watched a tear spill down his sunken cheek, and felt her own eyes well up in sympathy.

"Because we have to," she said firmly when she could be sure her voice wasn't going to wobble. "Because it's not fair to them otherwise."

Afterwards, she helped him back into the waiting room, where his mother leapt to her feet and hovered anxiously by his side.

"I've taken the stitches out and the wound is healing well, Mrs Joseph," Ellie said.

"Oh, thank you," the older woman replied, but she didn't take her eyes from her son. "Come on, Kit," she said with false cheer. "Let's get you home and out into this beautiful sunshine." She took his arm gingerly, as though afraid he might shatter, and they walked slowly from the surgery.

Ellie watched them go, the son still moving like a ghost with his mother looking as though she wanted to scoop him into her arms as she might have done when he was a child.

She was glad that she had a moment's break before she was due to go and see Mr Harris. She was so grateful for her work. It was keeping her busy, and that made it easier to prevent her mind from lingering on Jack: where he was, and what he was be doing; how soon he would be sent to France, and into danger; whether he was thinking of her or whether all his thoughts were with Maggie now; sadness that they hadn't had a chance to say goodbye... At least, the work prevented her mind from doing this *most* of the time.

Shaking off the thoughts as best she could, Ellie gathered her things into her work bag, pulled the front door of the surgery closed (doors in Endstone were rarely locked) and fetched her bicycle, before setting off out to Mr Harris's farm.

It was indeed a lovely summer's day and the back of Ellie's collar soon felt clammy. She cycled alongside the stream, wishing she could stop, take her shoes off and dip her feet in. By the time she had cycled down the path leading to Mr Harris's house, her hair had escaped its grips and was hanging in damp tendrils around her face. She repaired the damage as best she could, enjoying the feel of the breeze against the back of her neck, knocked and then walked in without waiting for a reply.

"Hello?" she called, walking through the dim hallway.

"In here," came Mr Harris's voice in reply from the living room.

She pushed the door and squinted in the poor light. Mr Harris was sitting by the window, reading. Dust motes danced in the beam of light that eked through the grubby window, and the room smelled faintly musty.

"Good afternoon, Ellie," Mr Harris said with a tired smile. "How are you today?"

"I'm very well, thank you. And yourself?"

"Ah, can't complain. The foot's feeling much better."

"Oh, good, I'm glad to hear it. Now, I think what you need more than anything is to get out into this glorious day. It's beautiful out there!"

"It looks it," he said with another small smile. "But I'm not sure how far I'd get on these wretched crutches."

"Well, that's fine. You were issued with a wheelchair, weren't you?"

"Yes, but..."

"But nothing. You need some sunshine and fresh air, and so do I. Let's go!"

He gave a chuckle. "You're a force to be reckoned with, aren't you?"

"I am," she said brightly. "I get that from my mother."

"Is that right?"

"Yes, it is. Now, where's the wheelchair?"

Ten minutes later, Ellie was bumping him along the path and out on to the dirt road, the muscles in her arms and legs straining.

"Oof, easy there, Nurse!" he protested. "Remind me never to let you behind the wheel of my tractor."

"Pssh," Ellie retorted with mock indignation. "I will remind you of no such thing! I'm sure I would make an excellent driver. I should love to drive a motorcar one day," she added wistfully.

Mr Harris laughed again. "And I'm sure you will, my dear. Or heaven help the fellow who tries to gainsay you!"

"Tell me more about the history of Endstone," Ellie said now. She had noticed that Mr Harris knew a great deal on the topic – his family had lived in the area for more than a hundred years – and talking about it seemed to inspire in him more energy than she saw at any other time. Now that his mobility was so limited, his mind often turned to his future, and that of the farm, and Ellie couldn't seem to think of anything reassuring to offer on that matter, so the more she could keep him talking on topics that distracted him, the better.

"What would you like to know?" he was asking now, his tone eager. "I've told you it has been inhabited since at least Roman times, haven't I? It seems to have been predominantly a fishing port back then, though of course we've never had the oysters Whitstable is so famous for. Some of the books I've read suggest that evidence of Saxon settlements has also been found here, and it was then that the region began to be used for salt production and coastal trading. Of course, that also means it has a long history of smuggling too..."

As he talked happily, Ellie pushed him past fields that were being worked by Land Army girls in their overalls and headscarves. She raised a hand to wave in response to their greeting, and then had to grab hold of the wheelchair's handles as it swerved.

"Sorry," she said, noticing that Mr Harris's brow has furrowed and his narrative had trailed off.

"Hmmm? Oh, not to worry," he replied distractedly.

"Is everything all right, Mr Harris?"

"Yes, yes, fine, really. It's just the sight of those girls there..."

"What about them?" Ellie asked, though she thought she might have a suspicion what was bothering him.

He made a harrumphing sound but didn't respond.

"Mr Harris?" Ellie prompted him gently.

"Well, some chaps from the trade board – agricultural organizers, I think they called themselves, something like that – came by the other day. Wanted me to let some of these young girls come and work on my land..."

Ellie waited for a moment, but when he didn't continue she said gently, "But isn't that rather a good idea? You said yourself that your sister is struggling to manage all the farm work."

He tutted. "It's our family farm. It's our inheritance, our history. If we just give it up now—"

"But it wouldn't be giving it up!" Ellie exclaimed, then softened her voice. She knew this was hard for him. "It really wouldn't be. Everyone's having to do it. And surely it's better than all your crops going to seed.

This way, the land can continue to produce, and when your brother-in-law comes home from war, he and your sister could take over again."

"And what about me, Ellie?" Mr Harris said sadly. "What do I do when it's all over, hmm?"

Ellie fell silent for a moment. There was no point in saying that, whether the land girls helped on his farm or not, he would never be able to manage the physical running of it again himself – he knew that. But she couldn't bear him feeling so purposeless, so useless, after everything he'd been through. Especially not when she was beginning to discover how much he had to offer.

"All those stories you know, all that history..." She said it aloud, but she was almost speaking to herself.

Still, he answered, with a wry smile. "Yes, if only there was a way of making a living from telling stories, eh?"

"Well, there's writing, I suppose. And teaching!" she suddenly said, stopping abruptly so that Mr Harris jolted forwards in his chair and had to grip on to the sides to prevent himself from spilling out.

"Whoa, there, Nelly!"

"Oops, sorry."

"Anyway," he continued, the muscles in his arms straining as he righted himself in his chair, "I believe the Endstone school is well supplied with teachers. They scarcely need more than two for such a small number of students."

"No," Ellie said ruefully, "I suppose not."

He reached back and patted her hand where it gripped the handle of the wheelchair. "Cheer up, lass. I'm not entirely a lost cause. I shall keep thinking."

After a while, they turned back for home. Arriving back at the farmhouse and pushing Mr Harris into the hallway, Ellie stopped the wheelchair in front of the large, dusty but grand mirror.

"Now, I bet you've worked up a bit of an appetite after all that exertion!" she said. "I'll make you some lunch before I go."

"Normally I'd say sitting in a chair is no sort of exertion at all, but the way you drive..." She swatted playfully at him and he grabbed her hand. "Thank you, my dear. You are a wonderful nurse. Just look at the colour in my cheeks!" He gestured towards the mirror. It was true: he was looking a lot less grey in complexion. "I haven't looked this hale since before the war. You do me a power of good."

She smiled at him. "It's my pleasure." And she meant it.

"Well, I don't know about that," he said teasingly. "I'm sure you much prefer looking after the young handsome soldiers rather than fusty old men like myself."

Ellie made a non-committal noise.

"Ah, but perhaps there's one young man in particular?" he said gently.

Ellie was horrified to feel her eyes fill with unexpected tears. "Come along," she said briskly, to disguise the wavering in her voice, "let's get you into the kitchen and sitting down with a nice cup of tea."

That evening, Ellie was in the sitting room with her mother after dinner. Mother was knitting by gas lamp, the blinds drawn tight. Ellie was leafing through the pages of a book Mr Harris had loaned her, but she couldn't seem to focus.

"My patient Mr Harris was asking about you today, Mother," she said suddenly, keen to distract herself from her thoughts with conversation.

Mother looked startled. "The poor man who lost a leg? Whatever was he asking about me for?"

Ellie stifled a smile at her mother's suspicious nature. "He just said he remembers you from church. And ... and Father, of course. He remembers Father and speaks very highly of him."

"Yes," Mother said, so quietly that Ellie had to strain to hear her. "Everyone who met your father speaks highly of him." She shook her head curtly. "But I can't think what the man remembers about me. And I certainly haven't seen him at church for a long time."

"Well, no, Mother," Ellie said, unable to contain a note of impatience. "He's an invalid. He's lost a leg." Mother flinched. "He lives out of town; he can't very well get to church, unless someone takes him in a carriage or is able to push him the three miles there in his wheelchair." She paused and made an effort to lighten her tone. "I think Reverend Chester goes to see him sometimes. But anyway," she went on thoughtfully, "it's no wonder he remembers you. He has an excellent memory. Everything and everyone are lodged in there for ever. He tells the most astonishing stories. It's just such a shame that he's stuck at home by himself and there's no one really to hear them."

"Yes," Mother said after a moment. "That is a pity."

Ellie reached over to pour the tea from the pot, as the two Phillips women lapsed back into silence.

NINE

AUGUST

Ellie was cycling down the hill towards the surgery one morning in August. There had been a heavy summer rain overnight, forming puddles in the dry and cracked ground, and she had to watch the path ahead carefully. So she was caught off-guard by the figure that darted out in front of her, emerging from the back of the church.

"Whoa," she cried, as she swerved to a halt.

"Sorry about that," called Anna Scott with a nervous giggle as she trotted to join Ellie. "I knew I had to hurry to catch you before you got to work, so I wasn't looking where I was going." She was still out of breath.

"Why did you have to catch me?" Ellie asked, panic cracking her voice, her hands wrapped tightly around the bicycle's handlebars. "What's happened? Have you heard something?"

"Oh!" Anna looked even more sheepish. "No – I didn't mean to alarm you."

Ellie felt herself frowning, even as a wave of relief washed over her. "Well, then, for goodness' sake, why did you—"

"I mean, we have heard something, but it's nothing to worry about," Anna went on in a hurry. "I've … I wanted to talk to you… Well, it's just… It's just that I've just been feeling guilty for teasing you about Maggie."

The name alone was enough to reinstate Ellie's scowl.

"I know, I know! But I didn't mean anything by it; it was only a joke." Anna was gabbling now. "Mam's been on at me to tell you that ever since. I thought she was making a fuss about nothing, but she reckoned it might have been the reason you didn't come round to say goodbye to him; the reason you've been avoiding the rest of us too. Jack keeps asking after you in his letters, so then Mam said maybe it was the reason you haven't been writing to him. Was it?" She gave Ellie a keen look.

"There were other reasons," Ellie said, a bit sniffily, swinging one leg off her bicycle.

"Look, Ellie, I shouldn't have said it, but it didn't occur to me for one moment that you'd take it seriously. Are you that daft that you don't know how Jack feels about you? It's only ever been you. Honestly, you should have seen him the night before he went away; he barely took his eyes from the door all evening."

Ellie's stomach gave a swoop. "But ... but, Maggie..." she said stupidly, her mind skittering all over the place.

"Oh, for heaven's sake!" Anna said, her hangdog demeanour giving way to one of impatience. "She was only ever a friend to him. I mean, don't get me wrong, that's not what she was after, and she certainly did her best to get her hands on him, I'll give her that..." She trailed off at the sight of Ellie's expression. "But, like I said, the poor girl could never hold a candle to you, as far as our Jack's concerned."

Ellie felt at a loss for words. "Well," she began again

at last. "So ... so, you said you'd heard from him? How ... how is he? He's not..." Icy dread trickled down the back of her head and spine. "He hasn't been sent to France, has he?"

"Of course not, you dotty thing!" Anna was back to her usual cocky self. Ellie narrowed her eyes. "Don't you know anything? They've only just started sending boys as young as eighteen and a half – which Jack isn't yet. *And* they have to have had at least six months' training. He's still in Folkestone!"

"Oh." Ellie was so relieved that she forgot to be annoyed.

"Still," Anna went on, her face falling once more, "that's only another four months, I suppose."

Ellie took a deep breath. "How's your mum?" she asked, feeling a sharp pang of guilt for neglecting the rest of the Scott family since Jack had gone away. He had always taken such good care of Mother and Charlie while she had been in Brighton.

"She's struggling, to be honest," Anna said, toying with her thick red plait. "We don't hear as much from Will these days, so she's anxious every moment between letters. And knowing that Jack will be following him soon..." Anna's voice seemed to get swallowed in her throat.

Ellie took one hand from the handlebars to reach out and pat Anna somewhat awkwardly on the arm. "Try not to worry. Both those boys are tough." She forced down the last of her annoyance and went on, "Thank you for telling me about Maggie, and about Jack's letter. I appreciate it. And please tell your mum I'll be round to see her soon."

"Yeah, I'm sorry again about Maggie," Anna replied. "But, oh, before you go..." She went scrabbling round in a pocket and withdrew a folded piece of paper. "You should write to him now, stop this nonsense." She handed Ellie the paper, but not before swatting her with it. "Honestly, Ellie, don't leave him hanging on again..."

"I don't know what you mean," Ellie said airily, hating how much like Mother she sometimes ended up sounding when she spoke to Anna Scott.

Anna laughed. "Yes, you do. I'll see you, Ellie."

Ellie watched her go, shaking her head. How had that girl managed to get the last word when *she'd* come to apologize to Ellie? Checking her pocket watch, Ellie let out a yelp. She would be only just in time for her first appointment! She dragged her bicycle around the side of the surgery and then hurried in.

As she moved through her appointments and other tasks that morning, it was with a sense of a lightened burden. All her worries about Jack and Maggie had been based on nothing – well, based on some nonsense Anna Scott had made up. Anna had said so herself! She would write to Jack and things would be better; whatever happened next, at least they would be on the same side again, at least they would be facing things together.

But as the morning wore on, doubts began to sneak back in. If there was nothing going on between Jack and Maggie, why hadn't he tried harder to see her before he went away? Why hadn't *he* written to *her*?

Turning her back to the patients sitting quietly in the waiting room, Ellie leaned her head against the cool metal of the filing cabinet. She felt as though she were being driven insane by her thoughts, unable to take control of her brain. This wouldn't do.

Come on, she told herself, mouthing the words at the same time. *Pull yourself together!*

As she turned back to the desk, she heard the front door to the surgery open. She didn't look up, her finger running along the appointment ledger to see who was next. When she saw Christopher Joseph's name, she let out a deep sigh, and instantly berated herself for it. It was just that the poor man's desolation seemed to come off him in waves, as contagious as the influenza epidemic the newspapers said was sweeping parts of the country. What was worse, his loss of vision was spreading to his left eye now. Thomas believed that his head injury had damaged his optic nerve. It seemed very likely that he would lose his vision entirely.

But when she looked up to scan the waiting room, she couldn't see him at all. There was Miss Webb – again – and Stephen Chase's mother, no doubt in to collect more medication for him. Then a young, happy-looking couple with their heads close together, who could have nothing to do with—

She started, began to doubt her own eyesight. The young man of the couple was Christopher Joseph! And beside him, her hands wrapped around his, was Aggie Farrow, sister to Billie Farrow, Endstone's first victim to the war. Ellie hadn't seen Aggie since before she had moved to Brighton – in fact, since shortly after Billie's death – but she had heard that the older girl had joined the Land Army and had been working on farms in the countryside around Endstone, as well as further afield.

"Um, Private Joseph?" Ellie called, gathering herself together.

Christopher and Aggie both looked in her direction, though she could see that his gaze was unfocused. She walked towards them wearing a shy smile.

"Hello, Ellie," said Aggie. She looked much older than when Ellie had last seen her, but also much happier. Her expression was relaxed and content, and her hands did not release Christopher's. "I agreed with Mrs Joseph that I would bring Christopher in to see you today."

"It's good to see you, Aggie. And you, of course, Christopher." Ellie placed a hand gently on his shoulder. "Dr Pritchard would like to take a look at your eyes today." She tried to keep her tone level and reassuring, but it seemed as though she needn't have bothered. He just nodded calmly, moving closer to Aggie. "I'll go and make sure he's ready for us," Ellie continued.

Once they were all settled in the examination room – Aggie on a chair beside Christopher's – Ellie took a step back and watched the young couple.

Thomas was gathering various flash cards together, with which he intended to assess the extent of Christopher's loss of vision.

"Are you working near Endstone again, Aggie?" Ellie asked her.

"I am," Aggie replied. "I was over nearer to Ashford, but then I realized Kit was back when I was home on a visit..." She blushed and smiled. "It just seemed as though I should be closer to home." He squeezed her hand more tightly and beamed at her.

"Of course," Ellie said.

Then they all fell silent as Thomas began to show Christopher a selection of flashcards and quizzed him on the shapes and letters they depicted. After that, he shone a torch into the young soldier's eyes, and looked again at his head wound. All the while, Ellie took notes and passed Thomas things when he needed them.

At last Thomas sat back down, drawing his chair closer to the couple. Ellie hovered nearby. She knew that there was no good news to be offered.

"I'm terribly sorry, Private Joseph," Thomas said now, "but it would appear that there was damage to your optic nerve. I'm afraid to say, I believe the loss of sight will be permanent."

He put out a reassuring hand, but again Christopher merely nodded. "It's as we expected, isn't it?" he said, flashing Ellie a small smile. "It's all right, Doctor, I'm prepared."

"Well," said Thomas, "what an extraordinarily brave response! If there's any way you think we could assist you, do let us know. You might find a cane helpful, perhaps?"

"Yes, yes," the private agreed. "That sounds a good idea. But you've both already been wonderfully kind and helpful." Again, he turned his vague gaze in Ellie's direction and seemed to draw himself up. "What you said to me before, Ellie, it made a lot of difference." At first Ellie couldn't think what he meant. "About getting on with our lives," he prompted. "I think if that hadn't been in my head, I might not have agreed to Aggie visiting when she was home. It never occurred to me that she might still... With the way I am now... Well..." He trailed off happily.

"You silly goose," Aggie replied, and the warmth in her tone made Ellie want to weep.

"I'm sad that I can't see my lovely Aggie properly," Private Joseph went on, "and that I'll likely never be able to again. But I know us being together makes me one of the luckiest men alive. I'll do my best not to forget that again."

"We're getting married!" Aggie burst out, as though she couldn't contain it for a moment longer, wriggling her ring finger so they could see the simple band that flashed there.

"My grandmother's," the young man put in in a murmur, clearly catching the movement of her hand in his hazy vision.

"Just as soon as Kit is strong enough..."

"Oh, bother that!" he said. "I'm more than strong enough to wait for you at the top of the church and have everyone tell me how beautiful you are looking!"

They laughed together, as though they were alone in the room.

"That's wonderful," Thomas said, and though his voice was strong, Ellie could detect the pain in it. She took a step closer, her hands itching to reach out to him. "Really wonderful. Many congratulations to you both."

Ellie joined in with his warm remarks, and then took over for the rest of the appointment, assuring the private that she would order him a white cane and put him in touch with Blind Veterans, an organization that helped to support and rehabilitate men such as himself.

As she watched Christopher and Aggie walk off arm in arm, she was struck by how different the sight was from the one she had witnessed as he walked off with his mother just months before.

Returning to the examination room, she knocked gently before entering. Thomas was sitting at his desk, filling out a form, but she noticed the photograph of his wife Sarah was angled towards him, closer than usual.

"Are you all right?" she asked hesitantly.

"I'm fine, Ellie, I'm fine. They're a lovely young couple and they deserve their happiness. Goodness knows they've both been through enough." He gave her a sad smile. "It's just hard sometimes, you know. . ."

"I do know," she replied, stepping forward.

"But you mustn't worry about me," he said briskly, capping his pen. "I'm fine, Ellie, really. Now, I believe

Private Joseph was our last patient for the day, yes?"
Ellie nodded. "Then I think I'll be heading home. It's
been rather a long day." He smiled again. "Aren't they
all!"

"You know you're always welcome to join us for
dinner," Ellie said anxiously. "Mother and Charlie love
to see you."

"I know, Ellie, and I love to see them too. It's very
kind of you, but tonight I think I need my book and an
early night."

"All right, if you're sure?"

"I am, Ellie. Are you happy to lock up the surgery?"

"Of course." And she was.

After Thomas left, she hurried around tidying
things up ready for the next day, then locked the door
and leaped on to her bicycle. There was something
important she had to do right away.

TEN

Dear Jack,

I know this letter will seem to arrive out of the blue, given that I haven't written since you left for Folkestone or even spoken to you since your birthday. I'm sorry for that, and for so many other things. I have been an idiot, and wrong about everything, I realize now. You know how stubborn I can be, how good I am at refusing to see the wood for the trees. Please believe me that I have thought about you every moment since you left Endstone, missed you and worried about you.

I've been forcing myself to really think at last –

I know, always so late! – about why I got so upset and angry that you were going away again. Of course it goes without saying that I didn't want you to; I wanted you here and safe and with me. Whatever I believed at the beginning of the war, I think you know that I no longer believe that hundreds of thousands of men from all across the world – even India and America – fighting and killing each other can ever be the solution to anything. It seems to me that it can never be anything other than a monstrous waste. Losing Father and so many of our friends, treating the injuries that men return from the Front with, has made me utterly convinced of this.

But I know that you no longer feel the way you did at the start of the war either, that you signed up because you felt you had to rather than because you wanted to. I've asked myself what I would have done in your situation and I honestly think I might have become a conscientious objector. But that would have been my response, and not a perfect one at that. I understand why you couldn't do it – I think I always have.

*So when I'm really honest with myself
about why I allowed you to go away without
even saying goodbye to you, I'm afraid I
think it's because of your friend Maggie. You
were right; I was jealous – it was no bigger or
worthier motivation than that. I think perhaps
I misunderstood the situation between the two
of you, but that doesn't excuse anything and it
doesn't really matter in any case. I was rude to
her and distrustful of you when you have been
my most loyal, reliable and trustworthy friend
for all of my life. There aren't enough words
to tell you how sorry I am. I am thoroughly
ashamed of myself too. I suppose I couldn't bear
the thought of losing you, and then stupidly
drove you away myself. Typical Ellie wrong-
headedness!*

*I hope you can forgive me, but I understand
if I've let you down too many times now and
have allowed things go too far. Please know that
whatever you decide, I will always be waiting
at home for you, maybe in our clearing in the
woods or our nook in the cliffs, thinking of you,*

loving you and wishing with all my might for
you to be safe and well and happy. It's what you
deserve.

Take good care of yourself, Jack. You are
precious to more people than just your stupid
Ellie.

All my love,
Ellie

Ellie lowered her pen and pressed the heels of her hands to her eye sockets. She felt exhausted and raw, but also relieved, as though a physical ache that had been niggling away at her for months had suddenly been removed. She gazed out of the bedroom window towards the cliffs. She couldn't see the grey waves crashing against the base of them, but she could picture them, could almost fancy that the sound carried on the warm breeze. She followed the line of the cliff in her mind's eye, from that swirling, churning base, up and up and up the crumbling rock to the small nook she and Jack liked to shelter in together. There they were, facing each other, their long, grown-up legs entangled where once upon a time they had fitted so comfortably side by side, with space for all the supplies they had deemed essential too.

Ellie tried to imagine what Jack would be doing at that moment, at his training camp in Folkestone. It was so strange not to know the details of his days, not to be able to recall some of his recent stories to help build up the picture, because she hadn't heard any. After checking that the ink was dry, she carefully folded the letter, then sat with her hands pressed into it, as though the strength of her feelings might soak into the paper and be conveyed to Jack that way.

A sudden rap at the bedroom door startled her out of her daze. Mother was standing in the doorway, looking concerned. Ellie had the impression that she might have been there for some moments.

"Is everything all right, Eleanor?" she asked, eyeing the folded paper.

"Everything's fine, Mother," Ellie said, really meaning it. She gave her mother a tired smile.

"Well ... good. I wanted to ask you if you could keep an eye on Charlie for an hour or so, please?"

"Of course," Ellie said, noticing for the first time that Mother had her light summer jacket on and was holding her hat. Ellie couldn't remember the last time she'd seen either of these items. "You're going out?"

"Yes." Mother paused for a moment. "Well, I was looking at the end of that rabbit stew, thinking that we'd probably had more than enough of it ourselves, and that it will need eating by today or tomorrow at the latest or else it will have to be thrown away. I thought I would drop it round to your Mr Harris, since it sounds as though the family are struggling to take care of him as well as the farm, and *you* can't spend every waking moment there..."

"But, Mother," Ellie said, flabbergasted, "Mr Harris's farm is three miles away. It will take you for ever to walk there and you'll be exhausted! Never mind the return journey!"

"Yes, I know, that's why I thought I would take your bicycle."

"My ... *bicycle*?"

"Yes, whatever's the matter with that? You won't be needing it again yourself this evening, will you?"

"No, but..."

"Oh, for heaven's sake, Eleanor, I wish you could see your face! Anyone would think I was proposing to run away and join the circus! It's not as though I've never ridden a bicycle before!"

"Ha–have you?" Ellie asked timidly. She couldn't even imagine it.

"Of course I have!" Mother exploded, splashes of pink appearing instantaneously in her pale cheeks. "Do you think I didn't exist before you were born?"

"You know I don't think that, Mother, but—"

"I'll have you know that your father and I often went for bicycle rides and picnics when we were courting, and in the early days of our marriage."

"Oh," Ellie replied, the sudden image making her heart seem to wring itself like a sponge.

"Are you or are you not for ever telling me that I should get more fresh air," Mother went on, "and take exercise to help with my headaches and sickness?"

"I . . . am," Ellie said slowly.

"Not to mention telling me what feels like daily that we should all make an effort to take care of each other as a community now that the war has affected everyone so badly?"

"Yes. . ." Ellie hadn't realized she had been lecturing Mother on these topics with such regularity.

130

"And is it not a fine summer's evening?"

Ellie glanced again at the window, through which warm, yellow light was streaming. "It is..."

"Well, then, Nurse. I am simply doing as I'm bid. I should have thought you'd be happy!"

Ellie almost choked at the notion of her mother being biddable – and by her, of all people – but she simply said, "I am happy, Mother. It's a wonderful idea and I'm sure Mr Harris will be very pleased to see a face other than mine, and to have a chance to meet you properly. Just ... do be careful not to overexert yourself." She continued more loudly over Mother's noise of dismissal. "It is a long time since you have done any exercise of this sort and you don't want to tire yourself out."

"Yes, thank you, Eleanor," Mother replied with a sniff. "You may be a nurse but I am still the parent here. What's more, I am a grown woman and not inclined to go haring wildly around the countryside on that rattly bicycle of yours. I shall be back in time for supper."

Ellie bit back a smile. She stood and watched from the window until Mother appeared through the front door, emerging into the pinkish light of the garden, a lidded crockery pot held in her arms. She continued to watch as her mother carefully placed the pot into the basket at the front of the bicycle, tucking a tea towel around it as though it were a baby in a pram. As she struggled to get the bicycle upright, Ellie had to stop herself from dashing to help. It was rather a shocking sight for Ellie to witness her mother with her legs astride the frame, her long grey skirt bunched slightly to one side, her straw hat perched atop her head. Finally she watched as Mother began her stately – if wobbly – progress down the path that led from their front garden towards the centre of the village.

Ellie felt an unexpected dampness to her eyes and she found she was twisting a handkerchief between her hands though she had no recollection of having picked it up. If there was one good thing about this war, she told herself, it was the opportunities it presented, time and time again, for people you thought you knew inside out to surprise you.

She scrubbed at her eyes briskly, and suddenly called out, "Charlie? Where are you?"

His little voice answered her from the back garden. She pushed her letter roughly into an envelope, leaving it unsealed, then scribbled on to it the address that Anna had given her earlier, licked a stamp and affixed it to the front, and put it into a pocket of her skirt. Then she jogged down the stairs, seizing Charlie's jacket from the peg in the hallway as she passed.

She found him sitting in the garden, a mound of pebbles before him, a stick grasped in his muddy hand and his trousers covered in dirt.

"Come on, Charlie," she said brightly, pushing aside the thought of how horrified Mother would be if she could see him. "Put your jacket on. We're going to go and play on the beach until supper time."

Charlie looked unfazed as he stood, dropping the stick on to the pile of pebbles. He grumbled a little as she pushed his arms into the sleeves of his jacket, but then took her hand without further protest.

When they reached the steep path that led down to the seafront, Charlie began to pick up speed, and Ellie felt an answering tug in her own legs. They started to run, and soon they were stumbling and slipping a little on the loose stones that covered the path. By the time the path levelled out at the sea front, they were both out of breath, and the stiff sea breeze tore the remaining air from their lungs. The last of the day's light hit the water with a flare that left Ellie's eyes dazzled, and she felt a sharp pang of joy in her chest just at being alive. Seizing Charlie under the arms, she hefted his (these days fairly substantial) weight into the air and began to spin him around, faster and faster, the beach around them disappearing into a swirl of colour, until her eyes were blurred and they were both squealing. At last she stopped, staggering drunkenly with Charlie still in her arms, and they tottered over into a giggling heap on the damp shingle of Big Beach.

Charlie clambered back to his feet and began to run around, gathering pebbles according to a selection process that was unclear to her, seemingly recreating his stone pile from the back garden. Ellie looked out over the grey water that stretched all the way to France. Somewhere over there, Father's body still lay, far from home. But the thought didn't hurt Ellie as it had done once. She felt sure that the echoes of her father that really mattered were all back here: in his surgery; in the clearing in the woods where he had liked to read; in the Dog and Duck with his friends; in the minds of all the villagers who remembered him so fondly; in Charlie – yes, and in her too.

Now she looked north-east, towards Folkestone. Surely Jack would have finished his training for the day. Maybe he was sitting by the sea, looking out over the water and thinking of home. She squeezed her eyes shut and tried to send her thoughts along the coast to him. She imagined them as a golden fringe of light running along the shoreline, like the view from the top of the cliffs of the sunshine kissing the water's edge. Then she pulled the letter from her pocket, where it had already become a little crumpled. Stopping to roll up Charlie's trouser legs and remove his shoes and socks before he could go paddling, she began to cast around the shingle, looking for the perfect shell or stone. Having discarded a number of shells as too fragile, she selected a small grey stone with a creamy white line running through the middle of it, smoothed by years and years of Endstone seawater. She ran her thumb over its matt surface and closed her fist around it briefly, letting the warmth from her hand soak into it. Then she dropped it into the envelope and licked the flap before closing it. The corners were beginning to curl a little in the damp air. She and Charlie would take the long route home so that she could drop it into the postbox in the square. It would be collected first thing tomorrow and on its way to Jack without delay.

ELEVEN

OCTOBER

Having finished checking the baby's weight, size and reflexes, Ellie swaddled her back up in her cloth, tucking the folds in tight so that she felt snug and secure.

"There, now," Ellie cooed, lifting the infant into her arms. "There, aren't you just gorgeous?" She dropped her nose down to the top of the baby's head, the skin so soft and fragile feeling, and breathed in that delicious newborn smell that was like nothing else in the world. "Aren't you lovely?" she went on, rocking the child gently in her arms. It felt like no time at all since Charlie had been this size. How quickly things changed!

"Is everything all right, Nurse?" the wan but contented-looking woman in the bed asked anxiously.

"Oh, yes, Mrs Allen! Everything's just perfect; she's just perfect." Ellie laughed. "I'm only being greedy wanting to hold her for as long as possible." She leaned over and reluctantly passed the little bundle back into Mrs Allen's skinny arms, immediately feeling the absence in her own arms like a chill draught.

"She is, isn't she?" said the young mother, gazing down at the little wrinkled red face in awe. "I mean, I'm her mum so I would think that, but I'm sure she's the nicest baby I've seen!"

Ellie smiled. "And you're absolutely right! But you must give her a name or she's going to have a difficult time of it, no matter how bonny she is!"

Mrs Allen chuckled, still not taking her eyes from the baby's sleeping form. "I think I'm going to call her Eileen, after my mother-in-law. My husband will like that."

Mr Allen was away at the front, but he had been home on leave just over nine months ago. Ellie knew that Mrs Allen hadn't heard anything from him for some weeks now.

"I think that's a very pretty name for a very pretty little girl," she said softly. "Now, as I say, she looks in the very pink of health. And you've been managing to feed her all right so far, haven't you?"

"I have. Can't say as it's comfortable, but I think I'm getting the hang of it."

"Well done. You let me know if you think you'd like any more help with that. But in the meantime, make sure you're having plenty to eat and drink yourself," Ellie said, handing the young woman a mug of water as though to illustrate her point. "And try to sleep when the baby's sleeping, at least for the first couple of weeks, to give yourself time to recover from the labour."

"All right," Mrs Allen murmured, rubbing a thumb gently against her daughter's cheek. "It's been hard to sleep this last couple of days, though; I just want to look at her all the time."

Ellie laughed again, the woman's happiness infectious. "Well, that's understandable, but just try. Or you'll be exhausted by the time she starts to be a bit more demanding!"

"All right, Nurse," Mrs Allen said again. "And thanks so much for all your help."

"It's my pleasure," Ellie replied honestly. "Now, I'll just make you a quick cup of tea and maybe heat you up a bit of broth before I go."

Down in the tiny little kitchen, Ellie leaned her back against the table top while she waited for the kettle to boil and the saucepan of broth to begin to bubble. She was loving her work more and more, though the days were getting busier and longer and more challenging. There was so much to learn all the time, so much responsibility, forcing her to make important decisions for herself. But being able to help someone like Mrs Allen was so gratifying.

As the kettle began to whistle, she turned back to the stove, splashing hot water over the tea already waiting in the pot. She glanced up through the window as she did so, watching the brown leaves go scurrying over each other in the little alley that ran behind these terraced houses. Autumn was here in earnest. The months were passing. And still she had heard nothing from Jack.

Don't think about it, she told herself crossly as she clattered a spoon around in the pot. She had known there was a strong chance that he wouldn't be able to forgive her this time. She had turned her back on him when he needed her the most, and then had taken a very long time to even apologize. She had meant it when she said to him that she would understand if he had just had enough and also when she said that she would be waiting for him regardless.

She put the teapot, cup, strainer, milk jug and a mug of broth on to the tray and marched decisively back up the stairs.

But later as she rattled over the cobblestones of the village square on her bicycle, heading back to the surgery, she heard a voice calling her name. Stopping, she looked back and saw Anna Scott hurrying towards her, the apron she wore when working in the shop still about her waist, its strings flapping behind her.

"Hold up, there, Ellie," she puffed as she drew close. "A girl could wear herself out chasing after you all the time!"

Ellie waited as Anna caught up, the beginnings of a sense of misgiving starting deep in her gut. "Hello, Anna," was all she said.

"You haven't heard anything from Jack yet, have you?"

Trust Anna to ask her so bluntly when she was

trying to put it from her mind, Ellie thought in annoyance. "No," she replied, trying not to show how much it upset her.

Anna frowned. "Oh, for goodness' sake! If it's not one thing it's the other with you two! I don't know what he thinks he's playing at this time—"

"Anna," Ellie said in a strangled voice. "Was there something—"

"Oh, right, yes. You're in a hurry, I suppose?" She shot a questioning look at Ellie, who merely raised her arms in a gesture of helplessness. "Right, well, we have had another letter from him." Ellie tried to quash the instant stab of jealousy. Of course he would write to his family. That was only right. "Nothing much to report," Anna went on, "though he did say it's fairly definite he'll be shipping out in December, once he's old enough and has done his six months' training."

December. That was only two months away. And with the way time was speeding by these days, it would be here before they knew it.

Anna was playing with the string of her apron, the scowl still firmly in place. "I don't know how much more this ruddy war is going to take from my family before it's over." The all-too-familiar splashes of crimson, shared by all the Scotts, had appeared in her cheeks and the rims of her eyes were pink. "He's just another soldier to them, but he's *my* brother. Mine! And not the first one they've got their claws into either..." Ellie put out a comforting arm. Anna glanced at her hand where it rested on her own shoulder. "Anyway," she said with a sniff. "I just thought you'd want to know."

"I do, thank you for telling me."

"Though why the two of you always need someone else to go between you like some sort of messeng—"

"Thank you, Anna," Ellie said again, more loudly. "Try not to worry. December is still a little while off." Anna snorted and Ellie found it hard to disagree with the sentiment. "I must be getting back to the surgery, but I'll come and see you and Mabel in the shop later."

"All right, then. See you, Ellie."

Ellie remounted her bicycle, and set off again across the square.

Two months. Just two months before Jack would be back facing death and horrible injury every day. And they hadn't even said goodbye to each other. If anything happened to him…

At the surgery she tried to handle these useless, agonizing thoughts as she always did, by making herself as busy as possible. As Thomas treated a patient in the examination room, she settled herself at the front desk with a crate of medicine bottles that needed labelling. But the task wasn't as distracting as she needed it to be, and her mind had the upper hand. Time after time she smudged the label and had to throw it away and start again.

It was only when Thomas's concerned voice startled her with a low "Ellie?" that she realized she had talking softly to herself. "Is everything all right?" he asked.

"Fine!" she said brightly, too quickly to be convincing. "I'll just run to the washroom if you're here to keep an eye on things for the moment."

Before he had a chance to reply, she leaped to her feet, sending one of the little bottles rolling across the table and, without stopping to retrieve it, hurried from the room.

In front of the small mirror in the tiny washroom, Ellie noticed that her cheeks were flushed. She stared at herself critically. If a patient looked like this, she would say they were in acute pain, or suffering from high blood pressure, perhaps even a heart condition.

She ran the water and splashed her face. As she did so, she knocked the soap off the edge of the sink and sent it skidding over the floor. Then, as she bent to pick it up, she banged her head on the edge of the basin. Leaning her back against the wall, she clenched her hands into the tightest fists and opened her mouth in a silent scream.

Calm down, Ellie, she told herself, *calm down right now.*

So unfair, so unfair, so unfair, came the answering voice in her brain.

But was it unfair? Could it still be classed as unfairness when everyone she knew was going through the same thing? That was, in fact, the definition of fairness. Mrs Allen was happy with her baby, but she might never see her husband again. Thomas had lost Sarah. Christopher Joseph had found Aggie but lost his sight, lost so many friends. Ellie thought of the patient she had seen that morning, Mrs Brady, who had lost her husband and four sons to the war. Her youngest was still away fighting but there was nothing to say that he would return home safe simply because his poor mother had already suffered more than any one woman should. Thomas had prescribed her medication for the anxiety and to help her sleep, and there wasn't really a great deal more anyone could do.

Could Ellie really tell herself things were so much harder for her than for anyone else? Or was it just that she had made it so much worse for herself by her stubbornness?

That afternoon at Mr Harris's, though, she was still struggling to keep her feelings under control. She found it harder to concentrate on his stories, and kept tuning back in only to realize that she had missed crucial details.

As she put his lunchtime sandwiches before him, having cleared a space in the piles of books and paperwork that covered the table, he reached out for his water glass and knocked it to its side, spilling water all over his lunch and the papers.

"For heavens' sake!" she exploded, seizing the papers but only able to watch as the sandwiches made with precious rationed bread became sodden and inedible. "I don't know how you can live like this! The place is such a mess!"

She took the papers into the kitchen to dab them down with a tea towel – they looked to be lists of accounts. The wave of remorse was sudden and almost physically painful.

Hurrying back into the other room, she saw that Mr Harris was attempting to soak up more of the spilled water with his handkerchief. "I'm sorry—" he began.

But she was already speaking too: "I'm so sorry, that was completely inexcusable."

"No, it was my fault—"

"It was an accident—"

"I don't blame you for getting fed up with me—"

"I'm not, please don't ever think that—"

"Ellie," he said firmly, placing his hand over hers on the damp table. "Everyone loses their patience sometimes. It's only human nature."

"No, it's not," she said miserably. "I know how hard it is for you to keep on top of this place. You're doing the best you can. I should never lose my temper with you."

"And you never have done before. You're always an angel of calm and tolerance."

She gave a snuffly laugh. "Well, I'm glad you think so, but I am known for being rather ferocious. My friend Jack—" She broke off again and suddenly her throat was too thick to continue.

"Ellie?" Mr Harris asked gently.

"Oh…" Before she knew what was happening, huge, shuddering sobs were being torn out of her. She had no control over them. Her chest heaved and her throat burned and soon her ribs were aching.

She barely noticed Mr Harris leading her over to the armchair and pushing her gently into it, leaning heavily on his crutch all the while. She saw but hardly registered the knitted blanket he put over her before shuffling from the room. She knew she ought to feel embarrassed – how unprofessionally she was behaving! – but she couldn't bring herself to care. Instead she abandoned herself to weeping, curled up into a tiny ball on the chair and feeling as though she were a child again.

Several long moments later, Mr Harris returned to the room. In the hand that wasn't leaning on his crutch he was clutching a mug from which chocolatey-smelling tendrils of steam wafted. He placed this on the small table beside her, drew up a chair and, after rummaging in his jacket pocket, drew out a crumpled but clean handkerchief, which he passed to her.

"Now, then," he said, his voice warm and comforting, "I think maybe you'd better tell me all about this Jack fellow."

And so she did. It was hard to know where to start, so she went back to the beginning – the very beginning, when she and Jack had first become friends after playing together in the square after church one Sunday when they were very small. As she talked, she realized again that there wasn't a significant event in her life in which Jack hadn't featured, even by virtue of his absence, such as when he had been away at war.

"One of the things we always shared was wanting to get away from here, to go and see the world," she concluded. "But now we have both been away, and I realize – I'm *only now* realizing – that it doesn't matter where I go, where I am, if I'm not with him. I'm such an idiot; it took me so long to work it out! And I'm too late. I've left it too late." She buried her face in Mr Harris's soft handkerchief and blew her nose nosily. It took her a moment to recognize that the sound she could hear was his soft chuckles. She looked up at him incredulously.

"I'm sorry," he said when he caught her eye – but he was still laughing. "I really am sorry. But, Ellie, my dear, how old are you?"

"Seventeen," she mumbled.

His laugh became louder. "Oh, my poor girl, I promise you that at seventeen you haven't left it too late for anything!"

"But I have—"

"No, Ellie," he insisted. "We all make mistakes, realize things about ourselves only in our own good time. You *have* realized how you feel about Jack, and you've told him. There's nothing more you can do now but carry on with your good work – which you do so well – take care of the people in your life, and of yourself, and keep your eyes on your own goals. And all will turn out as it should, however that may be."

She looked up at him. It was so easy, with patients whose lives had been changed for ever by illness or injury, to feel as though they were victims, at the mercy of what the world had thrown at them. But, once again, here was someone who had every right to feel bitter and let-down, who instead was showing her the way through her own suffering.

"Do you think you can do that, Ellie?" he asked her now. His tone was gentle but it brooked no feeble protests.

She wiped her face with a dry corner of the handkerchief, drew her spine upright and looked him in the eye. "I can try. Yes. I can try."

TWELVE

NOVEMBER 11TH

Ellie was in the smaller examination room at the surgery. In truth, it was scarcely bigger than a cupboard, a fact that Miss Webb, her current patient, had mentioned at least four times in as many minutes.

"But I don't understand why we can't be in the main room," the cantankerous old spinster said again. "Why must we squeeze into this pantry?"

"Because," Ellie said patiently, "Dr Pritchard needs the main examination room himself."

"And I'm not as important as his patient, is that it?" Miss Webb snapped. "That's why I am only deemed worthy of being seen by a nurse rather than the real doctor?"

Ellie gritted her teeth. "Miss Webb, what can I do for you today? I'm sure you don't want to be cooped up in this little room for any longer than necessary." *Especially with a mere nurse,* she added to herself silently.

"No indeed." Miss Webb sniffed loudly. "Not in my condition. Anyway, it's about my blood pressure."

Ellie fought the urge to roll her eyes. "We checked your blood pressure last week," she reminded the old lady. "You thought it was low, remember? And, as it happened, it was perfectly fine."

"Yes, well, that was last week. I'm *sure* it's too high now. You must check it again."

"Very well," Ellie said, knowing there was no use in arguing. "What makes you think it's high?"

"Young lady, I know my own body! Do you think you get to my age without knowing a thing or two about your body?"

"I suppose not," Ellie said, reaching for the blood pressure monitor. The sooner she could give Miss Webb what she wanted, the sooner she would be gone and Ellie could get on with treating a patient who was actually sick. She felt guilty for wanting to get rid of her; she knew the poor woman was mostly lonely. But it was difficult to not to feel frustrated when so many others had very real need of medical help.

"Let's have a look then," she said, rolling up Miss Webb's cardigan, and the sleeve of the dark grey dress beneath. She wrapped the band around the soft skin of her upper arm and fastened it tightly.

"Careful!" Miss Webb groused.

"Sorry," Ellie said, beginning to squeeze the pump to tighten the band further.

"I'm sure I won't live to see the end of this war," Miss Webb said now, settling back into her chair; as always she seemed to feel better just by the fact of having her concerns taken seriously.

"Don't say that," Ellie said soothingly. "You're in fine health, Miss Webb. And you're made of sterner stuff than you think."

"Pah! How can you say that? Between my heart and my lungs, my headaches and my blood pressure… My stomach is not at all strong either. And my bones are very brittle. They ache so in the cold."

Ellie stopped squeezing and looked away to hide her smile. She wondered, were they to sit here long enough, if Miss Webb would name every organ, muscle and bone in her body.

Distantly, she heard the front door of the surgery crash open, and winced, thinking of the paintwork in the hallway. They tried to keep the place looking neat, but it was becoming harder with limited time and resources.

"And it's only got worse since the start of the war. You know that yourself. Why if your poor father were here today to see how I've declined..."

He would give you a dose of some sugar pills and a bit of sympathy, and send you on your way, just as he always did, Ellie thought to herself. She was dimly aware of raised voices in the waiting room and wondered if she ought to go out and check that there was no emergency. In the meantime, she glanced at the gauge on the monitor. Just as she had expected.

"There, now, Miss Webb. Your blood pressure is still perfectly normal. There is nothing at all for you to worry about."

"Hmm, are you sure you did it right? I *know* I've

been feeling peculiar. Perhaps we should get the doctor to ch—"

Just then, the door to the little room clanged open to reveal George Scott standing there, his face flushed and his copper curls wild.

"George?" Ellie began in alarm.

"Young man, what is the meaning of th—"

"War's over, Ellie!" George declared breathlessly. "It's over! The arm... Armstisstis... Arms..." He threw his arms up in frustration. Ellie found she was on her feet. "The peace has been signed! The old Kaiser has abdi... Well, he's gone. Run away or something. That's what. It's over!"

"Over?" Ellie asked, seizing his hands.

"Yes! Mam just got the papers in from London. It's really real. Will and Jack are going to come home! It's over." He paused for a moment, frowning. "I suppose I shall never be a soldier now." Then he shrugged, wrenched his hands free of hers and ran off.

Ellie was still standing, her hands outstretched where they had held his. The noises from the waiting room resolved themselves into cheers, sobs, shouts of joy and disbelief. Still Ellie stood. *Over...*

Ellie burst into movement and out of the room after George, only dimly aware of Miss Webb's plaintive cries behind her. Thomas was emerging from the main examination at the same time, looking ashen, his patient, yet another injured veteran, behind him.

Ellie wrapped her hands around his. "Thomas? Is it true?"

"I . . . I don't know, Ellie. I just—"

The shrill bell of the telephone on the main desk cut through the sounds in the waiting room. A sudden expectant hush descended. Thomas advanced towards the phone as though it might explode and stood looking at it for two more long rings before he answered.

"Yes? Yes, I'll hold, thank you, operator. . . Andrew? Is that. . . Yes, hello, old thing. . ."

Ellie stood with her patients in the waiting room. All eyes were on Thomas. It felt as though nobody were breathing, so still was the room around where he stood, as if spot-lit, grasping the telephone.

"That is jolly. . . That's. . . Yes, yes, of course. And you. Thank you, Andrew, thank you." He placed the telephone back into its cradle and stood for long seconds, looking at it.

"Thomas?" Ellie asked at last, unable to contain herself any longer.

He looked up, his face still pale, and glanced around at the faces pointed towards him. "It's true," he said, his voice scarcely above a whisper. "It's true. It's over. The Germans have surrendered."

The response was an explosion of sound. Spontaneous cries burst forth; embraces were shared; some ran from the room; others stood, looking dazed. Thomas sank down into the seat behind the front desk, still staring at the telephone.

Ellie stepped behind him and put a hand on his shoulder. He looked up at her and smiled. "Your Jack will be coming home, Ellie. He'll come home."

"Yes." She returned his smile, giving his shoulder a squeeze.

The waiting room was emptying out now, though many stopped to shake Ellie's and Thomas's hands, to offer them kisses on the cheek, as they left.

"If it's not too much trouble," came a sour voice from behind Ellie, "might you please remove this wretched device? It's rather uncomfortable, you know!"

"Miss Webb!" Ellie exclaimed, hastening to

unfasten the blood pressure monitor. "I'm so sorry."
She removed the monitor and Miss Webb released a gale
of a sigh. "But isn't it wonderful news?"

Miss Webb sniffed once more. "I suppose so, child,
but really, there's no call for you to neglect your work!
And it doesn't change a thing in terms of my health,
you know..."

Ellie couldn't help it – she burst out laughing. She
heard Thomas's answering snort behind her and that
only made things worse. Soon the pair of them were
breathless with laughter, dabbing ineffectually at their
eyes, while Miss Webb looked on with a mystified and
increasingly irate expression.

"I don't see what's in the least bit amusing about my
health. Whatever has come over the pair of you? Well,
really, this is just..." She spluttered to a halt, then,
drawing her shawl about her and tossing her head,
turned and marched towards the door.

"Miss Webb!" Ellie gasped behind her, struggling to
draw breath. "I'm sorry! I'm sorry! I'll call in to check
on you tomorrow..."

But the old woman was gone and Ellie and Thomas
gave themselves over to their laughter.

When they finally subsided, wiping at tears that suddenly didn't seem to be attributable to the laughter, Thomas looked up at her once more.

"This is wonderful news, Ellie. You should be with your family. And you should go and see the Scotts too. I don't imagine we'll have any other patients this afternoon."

"Yes, you're right. But, Thomas, please come round and have dinner with us. No one should be alone today."

He paused for a moment, then said, "Yes. Yes, all right, then; that would be lovely. I might go home, and maybe visit Sarah's grave first. I feel we should be together, in whatever strange way, today."

"Do that," Ellie said, feeling that familiar dragging in her chest. "Why don't you go now? I'll close up here."

"All right," Thomas said again. "Thank you, Ellie."

It felt eerily quiet in the surgery after he'd gone and Ellie wasn't inclined to linger. She rushed around putting away the medicines and confidential paperwork, then shut the surgery up and hurried on to her bicycle.

She knew she ought to get home as quickly as possible – she wanted to – but Thomas's words were still in her mind, and she felt desperate to share this moment with Jack's family – the other people who would understand its precise significance to her. So she detoured via the village square, where the atmosphere couldn't have been more different from the stillness in the surgery.

Already the square was filling up, and crowds were spilling in and out of the Dog and Duck. The church bells were ringing and there was a festival feeling in the air. It reminded Ellie oddly of the scenes when war had first broken out, four long years previously, except that there were far fewer men, and many of the ones who were there were horribly injured. Now, among the celebration and music and dancing, many stood weeping as they embraced one another, or simply stared exhaustedly into the middle distance.

Ellie saw Mabel and Anna Scott among the throngs in front of their store. She abandoned her bicycle on the ground and fought her way through to them, stopping to clasp hands and share exclamations of joy and disbelief on her route.

Mabel and Anna stood close together, arms about each other's waists. Mabel was openly weeping but her face broke into a wobbly smile when she saw Ellie. She loosed one arm from about her daughter and extended it to Ellie. Ellie stepped silently into it, and for a long moment they stood together like this.

"My boys. . ." Mabel said at last.

"They're coming home," Ellie said croakily. "They're going to be safe!"

Ellie knew that there had been no word from Will for some time, and she was certain this was at the front of Mabel's mind. But surely the lack of news was itself a good sign; now that the fighting had ended, he must be safe?

Mrs Baker had brought out bottles of wine and cider and beer and was passing them around the villagers. Mabel gave a sniff and, releasing both girls, wiped her hands over her face. "We should see what we can bring out from the shop, Anna. Maybe rustle up some corned beef sandwiches or something."

"There's the fish paste too, Mam," Anna said, with something approaching her usual briskness.

"Yes, good idea," Mabel replied.

"I should go," Ellie said, shaking her head to the glass of cider proffered by Mrs Baker.

"You're not staying?" Anna asked in surprise.

"No, I should get back to Mother and Charlie."

Anna looked as though she might disagree, but Mabel cut in with: "Of course you must. Give them our love, and perhaps you might all come into the village together later."

"Perhaps," Ellie said doubtfully.

She took her leave of the Scotts and then battled back through the crowds to retrieve her bicycle. She spotted Maggie in the swarm of bodies. The other girl looked at her and raised an eyebrow, giving her a knowing smile. Ellie forced herself to nod, but then looked away quickly as Maggie hurried forward to speak with Mabel and Anna.

Ellie cycled home faster than she had ever done before, and was panting heavily by the time she burst in through the front door. Charlie cannoned straight into her legs, giggling in a way that soon set her off too. The church bells were audible, along with the distant hubbub from the square, but otherwise the house was still.

"Mother?" Ellie called.

"Here," Mother replied softly. Ellie walked into the

kitchen and saw her sitting there calmly, a full but cold-looking cup of tea before her.

"Mother?" Ellie said again in surprise. "Haven't you heard? It's over! The armistice has been agreed! The war is over."

"It's over," Mother agreed. "Yes, I have heard." She gave Ellie a small smile.

"But..." Ellie trailed off, looking at her mother's slight form. She disentangled Charlie from around her legs and sat down opposite her, pulling her little brother into her lap instead. She heaved a deep breath. "Father..." was all she said.

It was enough. "Yes," Mother replied, and for a moment her face creased with such pain that Ellie's hand darted out automatically to grab her mother's.

They sat like this for a moment, until Charlie, looking utterly perplexed, began to squirm and whine to be released. The ensuing scuffle as Ellie lowered him to the floor seemed to shake Mother from her thoughts.

"It is wonderful news," she said. "Thank God. Thank God."

"Yes," Ellie said, smiling as she watched Charlie tear off again.

But a new and sudden thought caused her stomach to lurch and her face to fall once more. Yes, Jack was coming home. Yes, against all odds, he would be safe. But she still hadn't had any response to the letter she had sent him back in the summer. She had been imagining him returning to *her* – to the way things had once been between them – and now she know that would not be.

Mother, misinterpreting her expression, reached out a hand to her. "Your father would want us to be happy now, Ellie. He would want us to go on with our lives, to live good ones. Why, if he were here, you know he'd be trying to persuade us to go down to the village and celebrate with the others."

Ellie smiled. "That's true. Would you like to?"

Mother grimaced slightly. "I'd rather stay here, if it's all the same to you. You and Charlie may go, of course."

"That's all right; we'll stay with you. But, I hope you don't mind – I invited Thomas to join us for dinner."

"Of course I don't mind," Mother replied, with uncharacteristic vehemence. "Of course he must join us. Let's see what we have in the pantry – you can help me prepare something."

And so Ellie and her mother worked quietly together for the next hour, preparing a simple meal of grilled sardines with roasted vegetables and the last of the bread. It felt odd to Ellie to be behaving so normally, given the day that it was. But at the same time, the familiarity was comforting.

Thomas arrived with a bottle of Mrs Baker's plum wine, and they spent a pleasant evening, talking about what the terms of the peace treaty might be, and how long it would take for all the soldiers to be demobilized and returned home. As the bottle of wine neared its bottom, the conversation turned to their absent loved ones, about what their futures might hold now that a future was possible once more.

But in bed that night, Ellie wriggled and squirmed, throwing off the blankets despite the November chill, then tugging them back over her body. She told herself time and again that she ought simply to be grateful that Jack was returning – so many people knew tonight that they would never see their husband or son or sweetheart or brother or friend again.

Her mind wouldn't settle though. Would Jack return and no longer be her friend? Would they see each other, pass each other all the time and never speak again? No! She wouldn't allow him not to speak to her! But maybe ... maybe in giving up on *her*, Jack had realized how much easier his life would be with someone like Maggie – someone lively and warm; someone open in her admiration of him. Would she have to see them together, to know that it was no one's fault but her own that it was Maggie rather than her with whom he chose to be?

Once more she threw off the sheets in frustration. She wished she could light the lamp and read, drown out her own thoughts with someone else's. But Charlie was asleep in his bed across the room, snoring softly. If only the night would just end...

She reached for her pocket watch and squinted at it by the pale moonlight spilling through the gap between the curtains. It was only three in the morning! This was no good at all. As quietly as she could, she levered herself up from the bed, pulling on stockings and shoes, and throwing a cardigan over her nightgown.

Having tiptoed down the stairs, she grabbed her coat and scarf and wrapped them tightly about her. Then, moving painfully slowly so as not to let the floorboards or door release a creak, she crept from the house and out into the night.

Stumbling through the darkness, she made her way to the top of the cliffs, found a perch and, huddling deep in her coat, settled down to watch the waves, and to watch the sky until it slowly turned from darkest jet to inky indigo and then to a deep sapphire colour, at which point she roused her chilled, stiff limbs to clamber to her feet and hobble back home before anyone could notice her missing.

THIRTEEN

It was a few days later, and though the strange atmosphere of celebration and mourning continued, Ellie and Thomas had returned to work. People had not stopped needing their help simply because the war was over, as they remarked to one another often.

Ellie had had a long day of rounds, as well as appointments in the surgery. She had seen Mr Harris in the morning and, on a whim – thinking of that day when Mother had taken him the stew – had invited him to join them for dinner.

She was late home that evening, having taken a patient some medicine that had just arrived on a delivery from London, delayed, as so many things were, by the upheaval that news of the peace was causing all over the country.

As she pushed the front door open, she breathed in the smell of roasting potatoes and sighed with pleasure. She didn't really mind cooking these days, not as much she used to, but sometimes when she got in from work, she was just too tired, and thought with longing of Mrs Joyce's hot meals in her lodgings in Brighton.

But her contentment didn't last long; Mother came storming from the living room and seized her by the elbow, marching her into the kitchen.

"What were you thinking, inviting Mr Harris round for dinner and not even telling me?" she hissed.

"Oh—" Ellie began, remembering with a jolt.

"Well, you might say *oh*! I hadn't anything in! I had to send Charlie down to the harbour to buy some fish before the fishermen closed up for the day, for goodness' sake!"

Ellie's eyes widened at the thought of Charlie trotting down the hill to the harbour alone. "I'm sorry, Mother, I forgot that I'd said to Mr Harris to come today. I meant to pick something up on my way home—"

"Really, Ellie," Mother said, red spots still emblazoned on her cheeks, "you can be so thoughtless."

"I'm sorry!" Ellie said again. She was annoyed with

herself for forgetting, but she could also feel the familiar irritation with her mother beginning its insidious progress through her mind. "But I thought you said you had a nice conversation with him that time you went over with the stew."

"Well, yes, I did, but that—"

"And I thought you wanted his advice on the vegetable patches," Ellie continued, sensing, and pressing, her slim advantage.

"Yes, but that doesn't—"

"We had such a nice time when Thomas came round the other night."

"Ellie!" Mother was the one to interrupt this time. "Enough! All these things may be true but—"

A polite throat-clearing from the doorway cut across their exchange more effectively than any alarm could have done. Mr Harris stood there, leaning heavily on his crutch. "Mrs Phillips," he said in his soft voice, "I completely forgot to give you this blackberry preserve I brought. My sister makes it. It's really rather good." He held a jar out in the hand that wasn't holding the crutch and smiled at Ellie. "Hello, my dear. I thought I heard your voice."

Ellie felt her cheeks flare. "Hello, Mr Harris," she said. With a brief but pointed glance at her mother, she went on, "I'm so glad you could join us this evening. And thank you for the preserve. Blackberries are Charlie's favourite, aren't they, Mother?"

"Yes," her mother replied, rather stiffly. "It's very kind of you, Mr Harris."

He chuckled in reply. "A very spirited young fellow," was all he said.

"Oh!" Mother responded now. "I do hope he hasn't been bothering you. He can be terribly talkative. I really don't know where he gets it from."

"Not at all," Mr Harris said. "It's been a delight to speak with..." He broke off, laughing. "Well, to listen to him."

Ellie grinned and even Mother gave a tentative smile.

"I'm sorry, Mr Harris," Mother said again, shooting her own steely look at Ellie, "dinner won't be a grand affair."

"Oh goodness," he said, "I'm not one for fancy cuisine. It's very kind of you to have me, and I do hope you haven't gone to any trouble." Ellie and her mother both made loud noises of protest. "I confess I couldn't resist a chance to enjoy another meal by the maker of that delicious rabbit stew."

"Oh," Mother said, and Ellie grinned to see how discombobulated she was by the compliment.

"And I've been having some thoughts about what you can plant in those vegetable patches of yours before springtime," the farmer went on. "Perhaps I could compensate you for your kind hospitality with some winter lettuce hearts." He withdrew a brown paper bag from his pocket and proffered it.

Ellie felt her heart contract and watched her mother fiercely, relieved when she darted forward to take it from him with a hurried, "That's very good of you, Mr Harris. I shall plant them in the next few days, if you agree? But, really, no compensation is necessary. It will just be a simple meal, and you are very welcome."

Ellie released a breath she hadn't known she was holding. She ushered them back towards the living room as they began to discuss the best times and methods for the planting of winter lettuce. As they settled into their seats, she mumbled, "I'll bring the dinner out in a moment," but her mother gave her only the briefest of nods before returning to her conversation.

The atmosphere continued to lighten as they ate their meal, and Ellie marvelled at how adept Mr Harris was at keeping the conversation going, at how interested he seemed in what each of them had to say, including Charlie. It was such a change from the sombre and scarred man she had first met all those months ago.

Although her relationship with her mother had improved beyond all recognition, it also felt like a very long time since there had been anything like as jolly an atmosphere around the Phillips family table.

"Why you only got one leg?" Charlie asked suddenly and in ringing tones, cutting across the conversation and causing it to break off abruptly.

Ellie felt as though all the blood in her body were draining into her feet.

"Charlie!" she and her mother hissed in perfect unison and in matching tones of horror.

"That's all right," Mr Harris said, collecting himself quickly. "It's a reasonable question, isn't it? Well, young man," he said, ruffling Charlie's hair. "I lost it doing an important job."

"*Lost* it?" Charlie asked, agog.

"*Charlie!*" Ellie said through a moan, but Mr Harris just laughed again.

"Yes, that's a silly way of explaining it, isn't it? Makes me sound terribly careless. I hurt it, Charlie, hurt it very badly. The doctors couldn't fix it, and it was making the rest of me poorly, so they had to take it off, I'm afraid."

Charlie's eyes were like dinner plates. "Oh..."

Mr Harris adopted a thoughtful expression. "Maybe you'll let me have one of yours," he said, reaching under the table to tug at one of Charlie's scuffed shoes.

"No!" Charlie said with a gasp.

"No? Well, I call that mean! You've got two of them! Greedy, are you?"

Charlie was still looking sceptical, but a small smile started at the corner of his mouth.

"Yes, one of these legs would suit me very nicely, don't you think?"

"No!" Charlie squealed, but now he was giggling too.

"Oh, yes, I think I should look very handsome with one of those legs..."

Charlie's giggles were getting louder. Ellie felt herself begin to relax and saw her own expression mirrored on Mother's face.

They had finished eating and Ellie was preparing to clear the plates away and to offer tea when there was a sudden knock at the front door. Ellie froze. She and Mother stared at each other. It was rare for them to receive unexpected visitors, and the last four years had taught them that good news tended not to accompany surprise guests.

Mr Harris looked from one Phillips woman to the other. "Erm ... would you like me to..."

Charlie had clambered down from his chair and was clearly planning to take matters into his own hands. Ellie came to and hurried after him. She arrived in the hallway in time to see him stand on tiptoes to turn the handle and pull the door open.

For a moment, she didn't recognize the soldier who stood there, twisting his khaki-coloured cap between his hands. It was only when Charlie let out a squeal of delight – "Jack!" – that her brain caught up with what her eyes were seeing.

"Jack." She took a step forward as Charlie flung

himself forwards, wrapping his arms tight around Jack's waist.

"Well," Ellie heard herself saying, though her mind still felt as though it had stalled, "that *is* special treatment. No one else gets hugs from Charlie these days."

Jack had scooped her little brother up into his arms but his eyes met hers over the top of the blonde curls. "Ellie," he said, and his voice was so familiar – so exactly the same as it had always been – that Ellie felt her lungs squeeze tight, as though they were trying to crush her heart.

"Ellie?" came Mother's voice, from the living room, but as though reaching her from a hundred years and a thousand miles away.

"Charlie," Jack said slowly now, "it is so good to see you, my old mate. But right now I need a moment with your sister." He put him gently but firmly back on the ground. "Alone."

Charlie instantly began to protest, but they ignored him.

"Ellie?" Jack said questioningly, and held out his hand.

With a roaring sound in her ears, Ellie took it, and

they stepped on to the path together. Without further discussion, they began to walk, still hand in hand, towards the cliffs. Just this feeling of his hand in hers, just this, and Ellie felt more herself than she had in the longest time.

She didn't want to speak. Having longed to talk with him for so many months, now she found that nothing she could possibly say was worth interrupting the perfect peace of this moment for. She couldn't even bring herself to stop to acknowledge the scuff of small feet behind them.

But as they neared the clifftops, Jack stopped suddenly, and turned her so she was facing him, taking her other hand in his. She could feel him trembling, and it made her heart contract painfully.

"Ellie..." he said in a tone of wonder, as though he couldn't believe she was real. "I've missed you so much."

She squeezed his hands tighter, still reluctant to speak.

"I've thought about that argument, that stupid, stupid argument, every day since I last saw you."

She winced and found her voice. "No, I know, Jack. Don't..."

He was crying openly now. "I wish so much you had come to see me that night before I left. . ."

She felt a rush of panic so acute that she thought she might be sick. She dropped his hands and reached for his face, wiping his tears with her thumbs, feeling her own start from her eyes. "I'm sorry, I'm sorry, I'm sorry."

"Ellie, I don't want to ask, but I have to know. . . Do you still feel the same way you did then? Do you think you might ever be able to forgive me?"

She was so shocked that she stopped still, her hands on his warm cheeks. "'What. . . What do you mean, *me* forgive *you*?"

"I know how you felt about me leaving to join the army again, but now that it's over, I thought maybe—"

"Jack," Ellie said, cutting across him. "You know I don't think there's anything for me to forgive. When you didn't reply to my letter, I thought—"

"What letter?" he asked with a frown.

"My. . ." She shook her head. "My *letter*, Jack. The letter I sent you back in the summer. The hardest letter I've ever had to write. The letter in which I begged and begged for *you* to forgive *me*. When you didn't reply, I thought you must finally have had enough of me."

Jack's forehead was furrowed in utter bafflement. But as she watched, she saw a tiny hint of his normal humour begin to infuse his face. "Well," he said slowly, "that sounds like the best letter I never received in my whole life!"

"You never. . ."

"Never got it, El. Not a line."

They stared at each other, struggling to decide whether to laugh or cry.

"So . . . you wanted *me* to forgive *you*?" he prompted her at last.

She narrowed her eyes. "Well. . ."

"No, no. . . That's what I heard. You were quite clear on the matter. . ."

"Jack!" She swatted at him, but then seized him by the lapels of his khaki jacket. "Jack. . ." She pulled him close and they rested their foreheads together. This was home. *This* was peace.

His arms slipped around her waist. "I think we might be the biggest pair of idiots in England, you know."

She laughed, but felt tears spilling down her face at

the same time, cooling instantly in the icy wind from the cliffs. "I think you might be right about that."

"And you know what that means?" he asked, rocking her round in an ungainly sort of dance.

"What?"

"We're really only good for each other, and should never be inflicted on anyone else."

She snaked her arms tighter around his neck and stepped on to the toes of his heavy army boots, so that the dance became, if anything, even less elegant. "Right again, Private Scott."

"Well, then," he said, stopping moving suddenly and taking hold of her chin so that she had to look at him properly. "Marry me, would you, Ellie Phillips? I don't want to be without you ever again."

Her eyes were open wide now, looking straight into his cornflower-blue ones. "Marry you?" she repeated, her voice coming out in a whisper. "Has the good old Endstone air gone to your head?"

"I mean it, El," he said, suddenly serious – more serious than she had ever seen him. "I mean it. We don't have to get married right away. Or even for ages, if you don't want. You can get on with your nursing and I'll do. . . Well, who knows what I'll do now it's over – once I'm demobilized and allowed to come home properly, I mean – but it'll be something. I know what I want, though – I've always known. And it's you, whatever way you look at things."

Ellie was reminded of her own words – so similar – to Mr Harris, months ago. "You're what I want too, wherever I am, whatever I do. . ."

Jack's eyes shone with tears again. "Do you mean it?"

She shoved him lightly. "Of course I mean it!"

"So then you're saying. . ."

"Of course I'm saying yes!" She shoved him again, and this time he caught her and pulled her tightly into his arms. She felt his whole body shaking now they held each other close.

When at last she opened her eyes, she looked over Jack's shoulder in the direction of the house. There, pale in the moonlight, was the figure of her little brother, staring at her with an expression of pure bafflement.

He turned and ran back towards the house. As he ran, they heard him call, "Mama! Ellie's crying again! And I don't know why!"

Ellie's laughter found a rumbling echo deep in Jack's chest. He spun her round so that they were both facing out over the cliffs, his arms around her waist once more and his chin on her shoulder. Together, they watched the moonlight catch the tips of the waves that churned far below, and set them alight with a cold, white fire that repeated itself, smaller and smaller, all the way across the black sheet of the sea.